A FISH CALLED WANDA
The Screenplay

by John Cleese
Original Story by John Cleese and Charles Crichton

THEATRE BOOK PUBLISHERS
211 West 71 Street, New York, NY 10023

A FISH CALLED WANDA

Library of Congress Cataloging-in-Publication Data

Cleese, John.
  A Fish called Wanda.

  I. Crichton, Charles, 1910-   . II. Fish called Wanda.
(Motion picture) III. Title.
PN1997.F48   1988   822'.914   88-8115
ISBN 1-55783-033-9 (pbk.)

APPLAUSE THEATRE BOOK PUBLISHERS
211 West 71st St.
New York, NY 10023
(212) 595-4735

First Applause Printing, 1988

Cast

ARCHIE	John Cleese
WANDA	Jamie Lee Curtis
OTTO	Kevin Kline
KEN	Michael Palin
WENDY	Maria Aitken
GEORGE	Tom Georgeson
MRS COADY	Patricia Hayes
JUDGE	Geoffrey Palmer
PORTIA	Cynthia Caylor
CUSTOMER IN JEWELLER'S SHOP	Mark Elwes
MANAGER OF JEWELLER'S SHOP	Neville Phillips
INSPECTOR MARVIN	Peter Jonfield
BARTLETT	Ken Campbell
WARDER	Al Ashton
LOCKSMITH	Roger Hume
DAVIDSON	Roger Brierley
SIR JOHN	Llewellyn Rees
PERCIVAL	Michael Percival
MAGISTRATE	Kate Lansbury
COPPER	Robert Cavendish
ZEBEDEE	Andrew Maclachlan
VICAR	Roland MacLeod
MR JOHNSON	Jeremy Child
MRS JOHNSON	Pamela Miles
CHILD JOHNSON (13)	Tom Piggott Smith
CHILD JOHNSON (10)	Katherine John
CHILD JOHNSON (8)	Sophie Johnstone
NANNY	Kim Barclay
1ST JUNIOR BARRISTER (DEFENCE COUNSEL)	Sharon Twomey
2ND JUNIOR BARRISTER (DEFENCE COUNSEL)	Patrick Newman
CLERK OF COURT (OLD BAILEY)	David Simeon
STENOGRAPHER	Imogen Bickford-Smith
JUNIOR BARRISTER (PROSECUTION COUNSEL)	Tia Lee

POLICE OFFICER (OLD BAILEY)	Robert Putt
1ST PRISON OFFICER	Waydon Croft
2ND PRISON OFFICER	John Dixon
IRATE DRIVER	Anthony Pedley
HOTEL CLERK	Robert McBain
AIRLINE EMPLOYEE	Clare McIntyre
INDIAN CLEANER	Charu Bala Chokshi
HUTCHISON	Stephen Fry

1. Exterior. Tower Bridge. London. Morning.

MGM PRESENTS

2. Exterior. Lincoln's Inn Fields. Day.

Two female barristers in wigs cross the road.

A MICHAEL SHAMBERG
PROMINENT FEATURES
PRODUCTION

3. Interior. Law court. Day.

The court is in session. Archie Leach is summing up to the jury.

ARCHIE. And on that point, members of the jury, I rest my case.

He bows to the judge and solemnly sits down.

JOHN CLEESE

4. Exterior. Hatton Garden. Day.

The camera pans down from Diamond House to find a young lady coming out. She is smartly dressed, wearing a hat fit for Ascot. This is Wanda Gershwitz.

JAMIE LEE CURTIS

She looks around to make sure nobody is watching and then takes several rapid photographs with a camera built into the bottom of her handbag.

5. Interior. Otto's pad. Day.

On a bed in a Japanese-style basement room, Otto West is dozing in the lotus position. His alarm goes off. He sits up with a start, grabs his gun and shoots it.

KEVIN KLINE

Having silenced it, he settles back contentedly to read Friedrich Nietzsche's
Beyond Good and Evil.

6. Interior. Ken's room, George's flat. Day.

Sitting at a table in his bedroom, Ken Pile adjusts a model of a strongroom
which he is comparing with a photograph.

MICHAEL PALIN

He seems satisfied and as he gets up from the table we see, on the walls
behind him, several Animal Rights posters.

7. Interior. Living-room, George's flat. Day.

Ken is beside a tank full of tropical fish. He feeds them and, as we draw
nearer the tank, we notice among them some rare and strange-looking fish,
particularly a beautiful angel fish – groomed, triangular with a razor edge
to her. He bends down and looks at her adoringly.

KEN. Hallo, Wanda.

The camera lingers on these vivid vertebrates as we see the rest of the
credits:

A FISH CALLED WANDA

With
MARIA AITKEN
TOM GEORGESON

PATRICIA HAYES
GEOFFREY PALMER

Music by
JOHN DU PREZ

Production Designer
ROGER MURRAY-LEACH

Director of Photography
ALAN HUME B.S.C.

Film Editor
JOHN JYMPSON

Assistant Director
JONATHAN BENSON

Associate Producer
JOHN COMFORT

Executive Producers
STEVE ABBOTT
and
JOHN CLEESE

Story by
JOHN CLEESE
and
CHARLES CRICHTON

Written by
JOHN CLEESE

Produced by
MICHAEL SHAMBERG

Directed by
CHARLES CRICHTON

8. Interior. Living-room, George's flat. Day.

Ken is still feeding the fish. The door opens and the human Wanda enters. She has exchanged the smooth outfit of the opening sequence for the garb of a gangster's moll: imitation ocelot jacket and leather mini skirt. She is followed by Otto, dressed in black.

WANDA. Hi, Ken.

KEN. Hallo, Wwwanda.

WANDA. Ken, this is Otto.

OTTO. Hallo, Ken, Wanda's told me a lot about you. Hey! Great fish.

KEN. Oh, th-th-thank . . .

OTTO. A little squeeze of lemon, some tartare sauce, perfect . . .

Wanda raps Otto. Otto squeezes her boob. Ken turns.

WANDA. George back yet?

She makes for the kitchen.

KEN. Nnnno. He had to ggggo tttto the bbbb . . .
Otto stares at Ken, astonished. Ken looks at him.

Wwwwha . . .

OTTO. That's er, quite a stutter you've got there, Ken.
Ken is dumbstruck. Otto smiles at him.

It's all right, it doesn't bother me. So . . . George needs a weapons man, eh?

Ken looks sharply at Otto. Wanda calls from the kitchen.

WANDA. Cup of tea, Ken?

KEN. Yyyy . . .

OTTO. Yeah, he'd like one. I'd a good friend in the CIA had a stutter. Cost him his life, dammit.

The front door opens and George enters. Wanda runs to him from the kitchen.

WANDA. Hi, George.

She embraces him and he returns the affection with a squeeze of her bottom. Ken is hot on her heels.

KEN. Hallo, George. Get you a Scotch?

GEORGE. Yeah.

Ken scampers off. George eyes Otto.

WANDA. George, this is Otto.

GEORGE. . . . So . . . you're Wanda's brother.

OTTO. Good to be here, George. England is a fine country.

GEORGE. She tell you what we need?

Otto makes a rapid movement, causing a knife to appear in his hand, and then throws the knife so that it sticks perfectly between the eyes of an animal on one of Ken's posters in the alcove. Ken stares, horrified.

OTTO. Something like that?

GEORGE. *Something* like that.

Cut to:

9. Exterior. Archie's house. Day.

Wendy, Archie's wife, is sitting in a deckchair on the lawn reading Country Life. *Archie comes out of the house and walks down the garden towards her.*

ARCHIE. Hallo, Wendy.

No response.

Had a good day?

WENDY. I spend the morning trying to get the waste disposal man to come, have lunch with Marjorie Brooks who takes up the entire meal complaining about her husband, then I have to play three rubbers with Philippa Hunter and I come back here and Sanderson's have sent the wrong flowers . . .

ARCHIE. Oh no! . . . Would you like some tea?

WENDY. Yes.

ARCHIE. . . . I won the case.

WENDY. This is the first moment I've had to myself all day.

Cut to:

10. Interior. Kitchen, Archie's house. Day.

Portia, Archie's teenage daughter, is at the fridge, in full riding gear. Archie enters the kitchen.

ARCHIE. Hallo, Portia. How was the show?

PORTIA. Awful, Daddy. I've got to have a new horse.

ARCHIE. I thought you liked Phantom.

PORTIA. He's not fit for dog meat. Can I change him please, Dad? It's absolutely vital and it won't cost much.

She pecks him on the cheek and moves off.

ARCHIE. Well, oughtn't we to ask Belinda if she could . . .

Wendy enters.

WENDY. I thought you were making the tea, Archie.

ARCHIE. Yes, I am, darling . . .

WENDY. I suppose I'd better get it.

ARCHIE. No, no, let me do it, please.

WENDY. No, *I'll* do it.

She starts getting it, noisily. She picks up a cup.

ARCHIE. I won the case . . .

WENDY. Oh! Now this is cracked.

Cut to:

11. Interior. Living-room, George's flat. Day.

The camera pulls back from Wanda, calculating, to reveal the four members of the gang sitting around a table covered with papers and models. George is giving instructions.

GEORGE. They're worth about a hundred thousand each. There are one hundred and thirty-five of them, that makes thirteen millions, my friends.

Wanda continues doing sums with her pocket calculator.

WANDA. Dollars or pounds?

GEORGE. Pounds, pet. This is the big one. So . . .

George looks at Wanda.

WANDA. . . . OK.

George looks at Ken, who nods. They all look at Otto. Pause.

GEORGE. Otto?

OTTO. Yes?

GEORGE. . . . OK?

OTTO. What?

GEORGE. The plan.

OTTO. Yeah! Great. No problem. What was the, er, middle thing – about the police?

GEORGE. We don't meet up at Heathrow until Tuesday because . . .

OTTO. Oh yeah, yeah . . .

GEORGE. I haven't finished yet . . . because the police will watch all the airports for seventy-two hours.

OTTO. I know, I know.

KEN. You wwwant mmme to ggget a bbb . . .

Otto is staring. Ken's stutter gets worse.

Bbbig . . . cccar . . . ffffor the . . . ggg . . . gggetaway?

GEORGE. Yes, Ken, a limo, OK? And put diplomatic plates on it. Right?

Ken rises, and goes to the fish.

OTTO. What if he has to say something during the break-in?

GEORGE. . . . Nobody says anything during the break in, Otto.

WANDA. It's OK, Otto. Ken's good.

GEORGE. So next week, we won't have to look for work and it won't have to look for us. (*to Wanda*) Oscar Wilde.

George leans over and kisses Wanda. Otto exudes malice, rises and crosses to Ken.

OTTO. You really like animals, don't you, Ken? What's the attraction?

KEN. Because you can ttt . . . ttt . . . trust them and they don't sh . . . sh . . . sh . . .

OTTO. Shit on you?

KEN. . . . Show off all the time.

OTTO. You know what Nietzsche said about them? He said they were God's second blunder. Bye, sis!

Otto walks to the door. Wanda leaves George and goes to show Otto out.

KEN. Wwwell, you ttttell him from me that I cccc . . .

OTTO. Bye George. (*to Wanda*) If you talk to Mum tell her I said hi.

WANDA. OK.

OTTO (*whispers*). Don't let him touch you.

WANDA (*whispers*). One more day we're together.

Otto leaves. Wanda goes to Ken.

WANDA. I'm sorry about my brother, Ken, I know he's insensitive. He's had a hard life, Dad used to beat him up.

Ken nods and, after a pause:

KEN. Good.

Cut to:

12. Interior. Jeweller's offices and strong room. Day.

Something violent is happening in a Hatton Garden establishment.

Employees are rising in alarm. They disappear from view when the reinforced glass of the office is splintered by a blast from a sawn-off shotgun. The gun swings round and shatters the lock of the office door.

Three balaclavaed figures burst through the door, pushing a terrified customer before them. The first (Otto) draws on a gun and fires two shots at TV cameras covering the room. A monitor on a desk in the foreground goes blank. Otto sweeps it from the desk. During these brief seconds the other two villains, George and Ken, have forced the terrified employees to lie on the floor, hands on their heads. Otto drags the startled Manager over to join the other employees on the floor and then moves swiftly to the steel grid of the strong room, producing a small cross-bow as he goes.

Otto is peering through the grill of the strong room. On the wall opposite to him is a small panel with a push button in its centre. Otto unhurriedly loads his bow with a bolt, thrusts the business end through the grid, takes careful aim at the button and fires. The bolt finds its target. The steel grill swings slowly open.

Otto replaces George guarding the employees. At the same moment Ken comes from the Manager's office and he and George enter the strong room where they start rifling through the safes, pulling out trays containing flashy-looking jewellery and tipping it on to the floor. After several rows of trays they find what they're looking for. Ken unwraps the tissue from a small package revealing two large, glittering uncut diamonds. They shovel the rest of these packets into money-belt type pouches.

All this is done with military precision and without a word spoken.

We intercut between George and Ken rifling the safes and Otto terrorizing his captives. He is unnecessarily vicious, delights in poking the muzzle of his gun into panic-stricken faces and intermittently amuses himself by vandalizing the office. He catches the Manager cautiously reaching for the secret button of an alarm bell, and forces him at gun point to stand erect. An apple from a lunchbox is placed on the Manager's head. Otto takes aim with his cross-bow.

George and Ken emerge from the strong room. George shoves Otto across towards the door of the Manager's office. The job is finished. George threatens the quaking staff with his shotgun.

GEORGE (*shouting*). Anybody moves and you're dead.

He blasts off a round from his gun.

George goes through the glass door of the Manager's office just as Otto vandalizes it. He is showered in splinters.

Cut to:

13. Exterior. Jeweller's. Day.

The three balaclavaed men run out on to a roof and clamber over the edge, making their way hurriedly down an emergency tubular fire escape.

Cut to:

14. Interior. Jeweller's. Day.

The apple drops off the Manager's head. Realizing that the gang have finally gone, he sounds the alarm bell.

Cut to:

15. Exterior. Street at bottom of fire escape. Day.

Emerging at the bottom, the three hurry across a narrow alleyway into the back of another building. Ken leads, pulling off his balaclava.

Cut to:

16. Exterior. Street. Hatton Garden. Day.

An old lady, Mrs Coady, is walking her three small dogs. Their leads get tangled up with a man on the pavement.

MRS COADY. Look where you're going . . . you chauvinist pig. Really, people here just think they own the pavement . . .

> *As she walks on, we notice a black Mercedes limo waiting at the kerb with the engine running. In the driver's seat sits Wanda, disguised in moustache, horn-rimmed dark glasses and chauffeur's uniform. She is watching the driving mirror intently. George, Otto and Ken cross the street, now dressed in business suits, and get into the car. Wanda accelerates away from the kerb but has to brake suddenly. They are all thrown forward and George stares through the windscreen, startled.*

> *Mrs Coady has frozen a few yards into the road, and is staring at him. Wanda swings the wheel and accelerates again round the old lady, just missing a dog. The limo hurries through the traffic. Ken's face stares out of the back window.*

> *Cut to:*

17. Exterior. London street (a quiet cul-de-sac). Day.

The limo screeches to a halt. The gang pile out of the car and run down some steps to a Mini Metro.

OTTO. That was *fun.* I love robbing the English. They're so polite.

KEN. The dddd . . .

GEORGE. What is it, Ken?

KEN. The ddddog.

WANDA. We didn't hit the dog, Ken, it's OK.

OTTO. Ha ha ha. Twenty million dollars and he's worried about an insect.

They are giving bits of clothing and disguise to Ken.

KEN. It's not ann n . . . nn . . .

OTTO. Stutter's not getting any better is it, Ken. Have you thought about surgery?

GEORGE. Shut up.

OTTO. Shut up.

George, Otto and Wanda get into the Metro. A police car screams by. Wanda peels off her moustache and hands it to Ken, who is holding a black dustbin liner full of their robbery clothes.

WANDA. Ken . . . bye.

The Metro roars off. Ken leaves in the other direction on his motorcycle.

Cut to:

18. Exterior. London street. Day.

Ken whizzes along on his moped, and as he passes a rubbish skip he tosses the black bag into it and speeds on.

Cut to:

19. Exterior and interior. Mews and garage. Day.

The Metro speeds along and turns into a lock-up garage. Otto closes the garage door as the others get out.

Inside, George opens a safe and throws in the pouches containing the diamonds. Wanda is removing the final traces of make-up with a tissue.

George shuts the safe door and fixes the combination.

GEORGE. Let's split.

OTTO. See you at Heathrow Airport on Tuesday.

GEORGE. No celebrating.

Otto leaves.

WANDA. No celebrating?

She kisses George.

GEORGE. See you in a couple of hours.

Wanda leaves. George comes out, closes the garage doors, sees Wanda departing, and goes off right, in the other direction. Otto's head appears from round a corner.

Wanda goes out, turns right and passes Otto, who is standing behind a wall. He observes George, who leaves in the other direction, and then follows Wanda.

For a moment, the mews is empty. Suddenly, a Mercedes sports car drives up. George gets out and goes back into the garage, shutting the door behind him.

Cut to:

20. Interior. Otto's pad. Day.

Wanda and Otto are celebrating. They kiss passionately.

WANDA. To twenty million!

OTTO. To a job well done.

WANDA. To us.

OTTO. To the best brother-and-sister team since . . . since . . .

WANDA. Romeo and Juliet?

They laugh.

OTTO. Could you believe those cockney klutzes bought our story? What morons!

WANDA. I want you to know something, Otto.

OTTO. What?

WANDA. Even if you were my brother, I'd still want to fuck you.

She kisses him.

Make the call.

OTTO. *Momento, carissima.*

WANDA. No.

OTTO. *Eventualle.*

WANDA. *No* Italian!

She reaches across the bed for the telephone.

OTTO. Hey. *Per comminciare, due insalate verde con peperoni, un linguine primavera . . .*

WANDA. No!! No!!! Make the call, Otto!

He starts dialling. Wanda writes on a piece of paper.

Are you really Italian?

OTTO. *Absolutamente. Si.* My name is Otto, it means eight. Say *arrivederci a Georgio.*

WANDA. Bye, George.

OTTO (*Italian accent*). Ah, yes, I wonda ifa you coulda putta me troo to da polees, *per favore.*

Wanda hits him.

OTTO (*immediately serious, impeccable English accent*). Yes, hello. Er, sorry to trouble you, but I thought it might interest you to know that the Hatton Garden robbery today was pulled off by a Mr George Thomason, who lives at . . .

He reads off the paper Wanda gives him.

Cut to:

21. Interior. Living-room, George's flat. Day.

OTTO. (OOV) . . . Flat 3, Kipling Mansions, Murray Road, London W9.

George hurries in, and calls out.

GEORGE. Wanda?

Nothing. George looks at his watch, perplexed. Then, going towards the window, he brushes something off his trousers. In doing so he cuts his finger. His trouser leg is covered in tiny particles of glass. As he does so, he hears a police siren. He glances out of the window and sees officers and a police car arriving. He hurries back towards the door of the flat, but is halted by a knocking.

VOICE. Police, open up . . . (*pause*) . . . come on, open up.

George freezes. His hand goes to his pocket and finds the safe-deposit box key. He holds it and looks around. He sees a small carton of fishfood by the tank, opens it, puts the key inside, runs to the window and, keeping low, lobs the carton out of the window as the knocking restarts.

Open the door or we'll knock it down.

George goes and opens the door. Three policemen are outside. One steps forward.

INSPECTOR MARVIN. George Francis Thomason?

Cut to:

22. Exterior. Road outside George's block. Day.

George is escorted down the front steps to the waiting police car. The camera pans across a passing canal boat to an American car from which Wanda and Otto have been watching the arrest. Wanda checks her bag.

WANDA. Passport . . . tickets . . . money.

Otto pulls out without looking and drives off fast in the opposite direction, banging the front corner of a car coming towards them and causing it to swerve violently across the road.

OTTO (*shouts*). Asshole!

A loud crash is heard.

Cut to:

23. Interior. Garage. Day.

Otto, with a stethoscope, is kneeling by the safe. Wanda hovers.

OTTO (*removing the stethoscope*). We're rich, Wanda.

WANDA. Yep.

OTTO. I bet these last two weeks with me have been the most exciting two weeks of your life.

WANDA. You said it.

He holds the door of the safe triumphantly. Wanda produces a cosh from her bag, holding it threateningly above the back of his head.

Otto opens the safe door. They stare in. It is empty. Wanda puts the cosh back into her bag.

OTTO (*breathing deeply*). OK . . . OK . . . (*shouting*) I'm disappointed.

Wanda is thinking.

Sonofabitch!

He gets up and starts kicking the Metro furiously.

What do you have to do in this life to make people trust you?

WANDA. Shut up.

Otto thumps the roof of the car.

OTTO. People are always taking advantage of me.

WANDA. Shut up and *think!* Where's he moved it?

Otto thinks, then draws his gun and fires two shots at the safe.

What are you doing?

OTTO. I'm thinking!!! Thinking what I'm gonna do to him. First I'll hang him up with piano wire, then I'll . . . where are you going?

WANDA. I'm going to talk to him.

OTTO. Then I'll . . . talk to who? . . . talk to *who?*

Cut to:

24. Interior. Room. Jail. Day.

Close up of George. He sits with his solicitor, Bartlett, and Archie.

ARCHIE. So in the course of installing these windows for your parents, you were kneeling on the floor, where there was broken glass, from the pane that you'd dropped.

GEORGE. That's right, sir.

ARCHIE. And your mother and father can confirm this?

BARTLETT. Yes, and his aunt, Georgina Thomason.

ARCHIE. Good, Bartlett.

There is a knock at the door.

Yes?

The door opens and a warder looks in.

WARDER. Sorry to interrupt, sir. Thomason, there's a young lady to see you.

BARTLETT (*to Archie*). Anything else?

ARCHIE. No, that's everything for the moment, thanks. You don't have to dash off, do you?

BARTLETT. No, no, no . . . absolutely not.

George rises and Bartlett goes with him.

(*to George, quietly*) George . . . Ken's got the fishfood. He'll be in later.

GEORGE (*delighted*). Thanks.

BARTLETT. *De nada.*

George leaves and Bartlett returns to Archie.

What do you think, Mr Leach?

ARCHIE. Well, I think we may be all right on the glass. But what else are they going to come up with . . .

25. Interior. Visiting-room. Jail. Day.

Wanda enters the room. Otto is some way behind. Several prisoners stare and whistle at her. George is sitting, looking impassive. Wanda sees him and runs to him.

WANDA. Oh, George . . .

She throws her arms around him and clings to him desperately.

My God, I can't believe this is happening.

A warder comes over to break them up.

WARDER. That's not allowed in here, Miss.

George tries to calm her down.

WANDA. Are you OK? George, I don't think I can handle this. I was so afraid to go to sleep last night. I thought the police were going to come and . . .

GEORGE. Leave it out, leave it out. OK. Now listen . . . listen . . . you stayed at my place, we slept late, you made me breakfast.

Wanda nods. George suddenly looks up and sees Otto, hovering.

WANDA. What?

GEORGE. . . . What's he doing here?

WANDA. He wanted to see you.

OTTO. Who did it, George? Kevin Delaney? (*sitting*) You want me to rub him out? Anything, you name it.

GEORGE. I have *friends* making enquiries . . .

OTTO. Good.

GEORGE (*speaking slowly and threateningly*). The jewels are very safe . . . if I get sent down it all gets handed back to cut my sentence. Now to cut my sentence even more, I could tell them who dunnit with me if I wasn't very happy about everything.

There is a silence. Wanda and Otto look at him, puzzled.

OTTO. Er . . . what was the middle thing?

GEORGE. Piss off.

Otto rises.

OTTO. Do you want me to spring you?

GEORGE. Now.

Shrugging, Otto moves off. Wanda is staring at George as Otto disappears.

WANDA. George . . . *you* don't think . . .?

GEORGE. Do you?

A pause.

WANDA. No! No . . . *No.*

GEORGE. OK.

WANDA. George . . .

GEORGE. What?

WANDA. Are you sure the garage is very safe?

GEORGE. Trust me.

26. Exterior. Jail. Main gate. Day.

Otto is waiting outside the jail. Wanda comes out, smiling charmingly at a solicitous warder who has opened the door for her.

WANDA (*to warder*). Thank you very much. Thanks a lot. Goodbye. Have a good day.

OTTO. So . . .?

WANDA. Well, he's not sure it was you. That's something, I guess.

OTTO. What about you?

WANDA. No, he believes me. That's why he can't figure out about you.

OTTO. Figure out what?

WANDA. Whether you turned him in or not, stupid.

Otto stops and turns on her.

OTTO. Don't ever ever *ever* call me stupid.

Wanda shrugs. They walk on. Wanda suddenly stops and stares ahead. Otto looks. He sees Bartlett and Archie walking ahead, talking.

OTTO. What?

WANDA. That's George's lawyer. The other guy must be the barrister.

Wanda starts hurrying.

OTTO. So?

Wanda takes off her leather jacket and gives it to Otto. She is wearing a low-cut denim dress. She starts towards Archie and Bartlett. Otto follows but Wanda checks him.

WANDA. Trust me.

She hurries ahead. Otto looks doubtful.

Archie and Bartlett reach Archie's car. They split up and Archie starts to fumble for his keys.

ARCHIE. Bartlett, you'll let me know if anything unexpected turns up?

BARTLETT. Yes, yes, of course.

They say goodbye. Wanda interrupts them.

WANDA. Excuse me?

Archie looks enquiringly at her. She dons a pair of horn-rimmed spectacles.

Don't I recognize you?

ARCHIE. No, no, I don't think so . . .

WANDA. Oh . . . But you are a famous barrister, aren't you?

ARCHIE. . . . Oh well, hardly.

WANDA. Well, could I have your autograph anyway?

Archie is very surprised.

ARCHIE. Er . . . yes. Yes, certainly.

He looks for pen and paper.

WANDA. Thanks. I'm studying aspects of your legal system. I'm American.

ARCHIE. Oh, really?

WANDA. Mm . . . I've only just started, though, it's fascinating.

ARCHIE (*indicating the prison*). What, er . . . what brings you here?

WANDA (*smiling so charmingly*). Oh, it's a little embarrassing . . . I have a friend . . . (*she indicates the prison*)

ARCHIE. Oh! Oh, I see (*laughs*) Well . . . there you are. (*he hands her the paper*)

WANDA. I knew it! You're Archie (*misreading*) Leash!

ARCHIE. Leach.

WANDA. Right. I saw you in court, er . . . two weeks ago.

ARCHIE. The casino break-in?

WANDA. Oh, you were great. Oh, I'm a big fan of yours. I love the way you, er . . . cross-examine.

Archie is surprised.

Oh, I really admire your work.

ARCHIE. Thank you.

For a moment they look at each other.

WANDA. Well . . . I'd better not keep you.

ARCHIE. Oh, fine. Right. Well . . .

WANDA (*clutching autograph*). Thank you for this. I'll treasure it.

A pause. They look at each other.

ARCHIE. Au revoir.

WANDA. You speak French too, huh?

She smiles at him and walks off. Archie gets into the car and looks in the mirror. Wanda glances back and smiles again. Archie drives away, his briefcase still on the roof of his car.

Wanda reaches Otto, who is waiting for her. He is suspicious.

OTTO. What's going on?

WANDA. Whatever George decides to do, he's going to tell Leach first.

OTTO. . . . Why?

WANDA. 'Cos he's his lawyer.

OTTO. Yeah, yeah, I *know* that!

WANDA. So I'm going to get to know Mr Leach.

OTTO. George is gonna tell him where the diamonds are?

WANDA. That's what I'm going to find out.

Otto looks nonplussed.

Cut to:

27. Interior. Visiting-room. Jail. Day.

We open on a close-up of Ken's hands holding the fish-food carton. He unscrews the lid, shows George the key and puts it back in. George leans forward.

GEORGE. You've done well, my son. Now, where are we going to hide it?

Ken leans forward and whispers. There are many visitors round them and George is checking his neighbours.

Very good. Don't tell Wanda anything. Otto might get something out of her. Now . . .

KEN (*with emotion*). George . . . you are ggggoing to get off, aren't you?

GEORGE. Sure. Don't worry about it, Ken. We'll fix it. Now . . . anything on Otto?

KEN. Nnnot yet.

GEORGE. You watch him.

Cut to:

28. Interior. Staircase, George's block. Day.

Otto lurks, suspiciously. At the top of the steps Wanda is opening the door to George's flat.

Cut to:

29. Interior. George's flat. Day.

Wanda opens the door and calls.

WANDA. Ken?

Silence.

OK. Looks like the police have been all over it. Let me just change clothes and then I'll help you look.

Otto enters. Wanda goes towards her bedroom. Otto surveys the scene. He sees the fish tank.

OTTO. Hallo, Kkkkken's pppets. Hey! Wake up! Wake up, limey fish!

He picks up a wire cleaning brush and starts splashing the water in the tank with it.

So how are you going to get friendly with this lawyer?

He stirs the tank.

WANDA (OOV). I don't know . . . I'll improvise.

OTTO (*stopping stirring*). Fucking insects. I thought Englishmen didn't like women, the way they talk.

WANDA. No, he's straight. He's kinda cute too in a pompous sort of way.

Otto is in the bedroom in a flash.

OTTO. You got the hots for him?

Wanda is in underwear, choosing a shirt to wear.

WANDA. I'm not into necrophilia, thanks.

OTTO. What is this, hump-a-limey week suddenly? Otto doesn't approve. Otto might get jealous. *E molto pericoloso, signorina, molto pericoloso.*

Wanda gets turned on. Otto throws her on the bed.

WANDA. Oh, speak it! Speak it!

OTTO. *Oh, carissima. Un ossobuco Milanese con piselli, un melanzana parmigiana con spinacci, dove'è la farmacia . . .*

WANDA. Oh, yes, yes, yes . . . no no no . . .

OTTO. *Si, si si.*

WANDA. No! No, Otto, not here . . .

OTTO. *La fontana di Trevi . . . mozarella . . . parmigiana . . . gorgonzola.*

They fall off the bed on to the floor. At that moment they hear the door to the flat opening. They freeze.

KEN (OOV). Wanda?

They remain motionless. Ken is at the main door, listening. Satisfied, he crosses to the tank and holds up the fishfood carton.

KEN (*whispering*). Look what I've got, Wanda. Treasure!

He shows the key to Wanda the fish. He notices the brush which Otto left in the tank and is puzzled.

Wanda, the girl, gets up from the floor and watches him, unseen, from the bedroom door. Otto cocks his gun. She motions to him to get back into the bathroom, and watches Ken put the key into a miniature treasure chest on the floor of the aquarium.

KEN (*to fish*). Ssshh!

As Ken starts to feed the fish, Wanda wanders out of the bedroom, casually towelling her hair. She feigns surprise when she sees him, and screams. Ken jumps.

WANDA. Oh my God, Ken, it's you. I thought it might have been the police again. Isn't it horrible about George. Oh, Ken. I have such a bad headache, could you run around to the corner and pick me up some aspirin or something?

She tries to steer him towards the door, but Ken hears a noise from the bathroom.

OTTO. (OOV) Shit.

KEN. What's that?

WANDA. That's my brother, he's using the bathroom.

KEN. Otto?

Ken's eyes flash with suspicion and dislike.

WANDA. Yes, we just went and saw George, oh, it was horrible, Ken, it was just horrible . . .

But Ken is already in the bedroom. He sees Otto, who is sitting on the lavatory, fully clothed. Otto gets up and flushes the chain.

KEN. Wwww . . .

OTTO. Isn't it terrible about George? When I find the bastard who squealed . . . I love that man.

KEN. Wwhat are you ddoing here?

OTTO. What am I doing here? Wanda was upset, Ken. She needed to talk to family.

KEN. She just had a sh . . . sh . . . shower.

Ken, looking around, sees the bed is slightly disturbed. Otto notes Ken's eyeline and takes his arm.

OTTO. I gotta speak to you.

KEN. Wwww . . .?

Otto leads Ken through the living-room. Wanda is sitting down, crying noisily.

OTTO. You OK now, sis?

WANDA (*sobbing*). Yeah, I'm fine, thanks for coming.

Ken does a take on Wanda's apparent mood change.

OTTO. Just call me if you need me again.

WANDA. OK, thanks.

Otto drags Ken out of the door. Ken looks back at Wanda, totally baffled.

Cut to:

30. Interior. Staircase. George's block. Day.

They come out on to the landing. Otto slams the door and pins Ken against the wall.

OTTO. What's the matter with you, Ken? Can't you think about her feelings?

KEN. . . . There's something ffffunny going on.

OTTO. Oh dear, oh dear, oh dear. You don't even know why
   you're excited, do you?

KEN. I saw the bbbed . . .

OTTO. Ken! Ken! Ken! I didn't want to say anything while
   George was around. But isn't it time you faced up to certain
   realities, Ken?

   Ken doesn't know what he's talking about.

   Come on! You're a very attractive man, Ken. You're smart,
   you've got wonderful bones, great eyes and you dress really
   interestingly.

KEN. . . . Wwwwhat are you . . .?

OTTO. We could have a lot of fun together, you and I. And I
   think we'd be really good for each other. What do you say?

   Ken finds it difficult to speak.

KEN. You mmmust be jjjjo—

OTTO. May I kiss you, Ken?

He leans towards Ken, who panics and starts running down the stairs.

KEN. No, you ffffucking can't.

OTTO. Just a peck. No tongue. Ken!

Otto down the stairs after Ken.

Cut to:

31. Interior. George's flat. Day.

*Close on Wanda by the fishtank. She puts the safe-deposit key into her
locket.*

Cut to:

32. Interior staircase. George's block. Day.

Otto manages to halt Ken by the lift door. Ken is breathing heavily.

OTTO. Ken! OK, you didn't realize I was gay. OK, no, look, I'm sorry, I've handled this badly. The physical side can wait, you need time but . . . will you think about it . . .?

Ken is rigid against the lift door. Otto kisses his own finger and then presses it gently against Ken's nose. Otto backs slowly away down the stairs. Ken stays motionless for a few seconds, then turns away, disgusted.

Cut to:

33. Interior. George's flat. Day.

Wanda goes and picks up the phone and feigns a conversation. The door opens and a shattered Ken enters. Wanda suddenly looks alarmed.

WANDA. Oh my God!

She stares at Ken. Ken is too distracted to have heard.

(*much louder*) Oh my God!!

She drops the phone. Ken looks towards her.

Ken! Somebody just called.

Ken is still not taking things in. Wanda, still dressed only in her shirt, starts pulling on a skirt.

They said the police know that the loot is in a garage in Fulham somewhere. You and I have to go get it, right now, Ken. We have to go move it before the police find out where it is.

She hurries him to the door.

KEN. Nnnn . . .

He pulls her back.

WANDA. What?

KEN. Nnnn . . . it's all right.

Wanda checks.

WANDA. What?!

KEN. It's all right! Ge . . . Ge . . .

WANDA. . . . George?

KEN (*nodding*). Mmmmm . . .

Wanda's brow is furrowed with concentration and anxiety.

WANDA. M . . . m . . . moved?

Wanda is astounded.

George . . . *moved* the *loot*?!

KEN. Yes.

Wanda grabs Ken and shakes him.

(*shouting*) Where did he move it, Ken? Where did he move it?!

KEN. Cccca . . .

Ken can't get a single consonant out. Wanda thinks. Suddenly she puts her arms around him and kisses him long and hard. Ken looks dazed and in a trance.

KEN. I don't know where it is. There's a key. I don't know what it's for. It's in the t . . .

Wanda puts her fingers to her lips.

WANDA. Don't tell me, it's better that you don't tell me. Oh you know, if it wasn't for George . . .

She kisses him again.

KEN. Otto tried to kkkkiss me.

WANDA. . . . I thought he might.

Cut to:

34. Interior. Locksmith's shop. Day.

A locksmith is examining the key through an eyeglass.

LOCKSMITH. No . . . nothing. No marks at all.

WANDA. But it is a safety-deposit box?

LOCKSMITH. Oh yes, but . . . could be any one in England. There are millions of them . . . hotels, banks, offices . . . sorry.

He hands the key back. Wanda replaces it in her locket.

WANDA. Thank you. (*she turns and, under her breath, mutters*) Fuck.

She goes out into the street.

Cut to:

35. Exterior. Prison yard. Day.

An identification parade. The old lady who witnessed the getaway, Mrs Coady, is walking along a line of men holding cards. She approaches George. The old lady spots him immediately, and says to the policeman, Ibsen, who accompanies her, and Inspector Marvin, who is watching:

MRS COADY. That's him. That's him, Inspector. He's the one who tried to murder my dogs.

Cut to:

36. Interior. Archie's chambers. Day.

Archie sits at his desk, working on a brief. Wanda comes into view outside. He gets up and pulls out a legal tome. As he does so he becomes aware of being watched. He looks out of the window. Wanda waves. Archie stares, then returns the wave. Wanda mouths, 'Can I see you.' Archie waves her round to the main door. He hurries across the room, opens the door on to the corridor and calls to his clerk.

ARCHIE. Davidson.

Davidson appears from his office.

There's an American legal student here, wants to see me for a moment. What time's Sir John due?

DAVIDSON. Half past twelve, sir.

ARCHIE. Right.

Davidson goes, and Archie hurries back to his room. He checks himself in the mirror and goes and sits at his desk.

Wanda hands her umbrella to Davidson and knocks at the door.

Come in.

She enters.

WANDA. Hi.

ARCHIE. How very nice to see you.

WANDA. Am I interrupting?

ARCHIE. Absolutely not.

WANDA. Really?

ARCHIE. No, no, really. Delighted to see you.

He offers his hand. Wanda takes it, then steps forward and kisses him on the cheek, which startles him.

WANDA. So . . . this is the place, huh? Very nice. I was over at the courts this morning. Boy, it's fascinating, so much to know.

ARCHIE. Really, you liked it?

She sees his wig lying beside the bookcase. She puts it on.

WANDA. Everybody wears these. Do you wear one?

ARCHIE. Ridiculous.

They laugh.

Well . . . um . . . I only have a few minutes before . . .

WANDA. Oh I'm sorry.

ARCHIE. But . . . until then, I'm all yours, as they say.

Wanda puts on her spectacles and sits. Archie goes round the desk to sit.

WANDA. I just have a couple of questions. Um . . . I'm having a little problem understanding preliminary criminal procedures.

ARCHIE. Good!

WANDA. What exactly is the committal?

ARCHIE. Ah, interesting. Well, er, basically it's a preliminary investigation where the prosecution presents prima facie evidence that the accused has a case to answer for trial.

As he speaks, Wanda runs an eye over the briefs on his desk for anything on George.

WANDA. Well, that's what it says in the books. Let's just take, for example . . . my friend George Thomason.

ARCHIE. Right.

WANDA. Now, when he goes for his committal on Wednesday . . .

ARCHIE. Thomason?

WANDA. Yes.

ARCHIE. George Thomason?

WANDA. Yes . . . do you know him?

ARCHIE. I'm defending him!

Archie is rather pleased.

WANDA. . . . What are you talking about? ·

ARCHIE. I'm his barrister – his lawyer.

WANDA. That's so great! That's so weird, though. Isn't that weird? Oh, I'm so happy it's you that's defending him.

ARCHIE (*taking the compliment a little eagerly*). Thank you.

WANDA. He's sure to get off now. Wow! I can watch you work now.

ARCHIE (*still grinning*). Please . . .

WANDA. Amazing . . . Well, anyway . . . at the committal George will plead . . .?

ARCHIE (*obviously*). Not guilty.

WANDA. Really?

ARCHIE. Oh yes, he . . . the evidence against him is largely circumstantial.

WANDA. But there was an identification, wasn't there?

ARCHIE. True, but a very . . . elderly lady. I think they've got the wrong man.

WANDA. . . . You don't think he did it?

ARCHIE. . . . No.

WANDA. Well, let's just say, for argument's sake, that you did think he did it.

Archie is a little confused.

ARCHIE. If further evidence against him came to light, for example . . .

WANDA. Right. You would then advise him to plead guilty and turn over the jewels to get his sentence cut. And he would turn them over to who . . . to you?

ARCHIE. . . . Theoretically. Yes, well . . . oh I'm so sorry, I've forgotten your name . . .

WANDA. Wanda.

ARCHIE. Wanda. What a fool, what a fool. Well, Wanda, there are really *three* . . .

A strange look comes over his face. It begins to dawn on him . . .

Not Wanda Gershwitz?

WANDA. Yes.

ARCHIE (*quietly*). Oh my God.

WANDA. What?

ARCHIE (*almost speechless*). You're his alibi! I can't talk to you.

WANDA. Why not?

ARCHIE. My dear young lady, you are a defence witness. (*he rises*) I'm sorry, I must ask you to leave immediately. I'm so sorry.

WANDA. What did I say?

ARCHIE. Well, it's not ethical for me to talk to a witness.

WANDA. Everybody does it in America.

ARCHIE. Well, not in England. It's strictly forbidden. Please, I must insist, otherwise I may have to give up the case. I'm sorry.

Please.

Wanda is looking at Archie oddly. She gets up and goes across to him.

WANDA. Oh, Archie . . . I didn't come here today to talk about boring criminal procedures.

Archie stares.

Come on, you know . . . you knew the minute I walked in here. I want you.

Archie experiences truly profound puzzlement.

ARCHIE. What?

The intercom buzzes. Archie answers it automatically.

Hallo?

DAVIDSON (OOV). Sir John is here.

ARCHIE. Right. Show him in please.

WANDA (*spelling it out*). I want you to make love with me.

DAVIDSON (OOV). Pardon?

ARCHIE. Nothing. Nothing.

WANDA. Will you take me to bed, Archie?

ARCHIE. . . . No. Sorry.

The door opens revealing Davidson and Sir John. Wanda kisses Archie full on the mouth.

WANDA. Bye, Uncle.

She walks out past Sir John.

Archie sees Sir John, who looks at him strangely.

ARCHIE. . . . Hi!

Cut to:

37. Exterior. Archie's chambers. Day.

As Wanda walks away, Archie's face appears at his window, staring after her.

Cut to:

38. Interior. Otto's pad. Night.

Otto is standing in front of a large mirror doing Tai-Chi with a Japanese sword to some loud Venetian gondolier music. Wanda lets herself in.

WANDA (*speaking loudly over the music*). He's pleading 'not guilty'. So you're safe until the trial. Leach doesn't think he did it. Ken says there's a safe-deposit box key but only George knows where it is.

Otto continues Tai-Chi.

Thank you, Wanda.

She stomps across the room and throws herself on the bed. She opens People *magazine.*

What have you found out?
OTTO. Not a lot . . .

WANDA. You realize he's in court tomorrow.

OTTO. I know. I know *that*!

WANDA. So nothing, huh?

OTTO (*about to thrust the sword into the chest of a dummy*). Nix, Zip. Diddly. (*he pauses in mid-swoop*) Niente.

Wanda reacts.

Cut to:

39. Interior. Archie's bedroom. Night.

Portia is complaining to Wendy, who sits at her dressing-table, smearing on cold cream.

PORTIA. Oh, it's too big . . .

WENDY. No it isn't, Portia.

PORTIA. It is, it's enormous.

WENDY. No it isn't.

PORTIA. Oh, please, mother.

WENDY. No, absolutely not.

PORTIA. I'm so miserable and you just don't care.

WENDY. Do shut up, Portia. All I get, all day, is people complaining to me.

Portia runs out. Archie is sitting on the bed reading a brief.

ARCHIE. Oh dear . . .

Cut to:

40. Interior. Otto's pad. Night.

Otto sniffs his armpit and undoes his belt buckle dramatically.

OTTO. *Ecco l'uomo.*

Cut to:

41. Interior. Archie's bedroom. Night.

Archie and Wendy, sitting on their individual single beds with their backs to one another, start to undress.

Cut to:

42. Interior. Otto's pad. Night.

Wanda takes off her jacket. Otto takes off his headband.

Cut to:

43. Interior, Archie's bedroom. Night.

Archie takes down his trousers.

Cut to:

44. Interior. Otto's pad. Night.

Wanda rips open her bodice, revealing a black bra.

OTTO. *Le due cupole grande della cattedrale di Milano.*

> *Wands falls back on the bed, sticking up a leather boot which Otto clasps with passion.*
>
> *Cut to:*

45. Interior. Archie's bedroom. Night.

Archie removes his shirt, revealing a slightly baggy vest. Wendy is folding her clothes neatly on the bed.

> *Cut to:*

46. Interior. Otto's pad. Night.

Otto pulls off Wanda's boot, puts it to his mouth and inflates it three times in ecstasy.

> *Cut to:*

47. Interior. Archie's house. Night.

Archie pulls off his short black socks and sniffs them. Wendy sprays deodorant under her arms.

> *Cut to:*

48. Interior. Otto's pad. Night.

Otto flagellates himself with the boot. He sniffs inspirationally under his own arm, then stretches forward and snaps off Wanda's black knickers, which he puts on his head.

OTTO. Benito Mussolini.

> *Cut to:*

49. Interior. Archie's house. Night.

Archie is clipping his toenails with a small pair of scissors. Then he starts attacking the hard skin on the ball of his foot.

    Cut to:

50. Interior. Otto's pad. Night.

Otto separates Wanda's legs with relish.

OTTO. *Dov'é il Vaticano?*

    He pounces forward on her.

    Cut to:

51. Interior. Archie's house. Night.

Wendy discreetly removes her knickers. Archie, reading a brief in his bed, yawns.

    Cut to:

52. Interior. Otto's pad. Night.

In the gloom, spectacular humping is taking place to the strains of Wagner.

OTTO. *Volare, eh oh. E cantare oh, oh . . .*

    His song comes to a premature end and a look of puzzled contentment spreads across his face.

    Cut to:

53. Interior. Archie's bedroom. Night.

Archie and Wendy are in their beds. Archie is deeply engrossed in his brief. Wendy is reading Horse and Hound. *She sighs.*

WENDY. Archie, I want you to speak to her about plastic surgery.

ARCHIE. Hhmm?

WENDY. Oh, I do wish you'd listen to me. I want you to speak to Portia.

ARCHIE. Oh! Right, I'll have a word with her in the morning.

WENDY. Good night, Archie.

No response. She turns out the light on her side.

Good night, Archie.

ARCHIE. Good night, Wanda.

Pause. Wendy's head comes back up.

WENDY. . . . Good night who?

ARCHIE. Oh, sorry, darling, just some stupid case I've got
tomorrow with some . . . lousy old hag . . .

Cut to:

54. Interior. Magistrate's court. Day.

*Wanda enters the courtroom, sufficiently disguised to be not immediately
recognisable. She sits on one of the public benches and looks over at George,
who is standing in the dock with a PC by him. Archie and Bartlett are
sitting at the front of the court, and Otto and Ken separately further back
among the public. The court is presided over by a woman stipendiary
magistrate, and run by the clerk of the court.*

CLERK. Are you George Francis Thomason, of Kipling Mansions,
Murray Avenue, London W9.

GEORGE. Yes, sir.

*Wanda catches George's eye and winks at him. He does a double-take
but then smiles.*

CLERK. The charge is one of armed robbery. Sit down, Mr
Thomason. Are we ready for a committal today, Mr Percival?

Percival, the prosecuting counsel, rises.

PERCIVAL. Yes, it will be under Section Six, Two, madam.

ARCHIE. That is correct – Six, Two.

PERCIVAL. Here are the statements, all to be fully bound, please.

MAGISTRATE. Stand up then, Mr Thomason. You are hereby

committed to stand trial at the Central Criminal Court.

PERCIVAL. There is some urgency about this case, madam, as the main witness, Mrs Eileen Coady, is elderly and has had serious heart difficulties recently; is there any possibility that this case might be put down for an early trial?

George now indicates to Ken that he wants to speak to him. Ken nods. Archie confers quietly with Bartlett.

CLERK. That will be for the Listing Office at the Old Bailey, Mr Percival. (*to the PC with George*) Take him down to the cell, please, would you, officer.

The copper with George stands and rummages for his keys. Ken darts forward. Otto, alert, watches. The magistrate and clerk converse privately. George says something to Ken and slips him a piece of paper. Otto's eyes narrow. The copper turns to take George out, and waves Ken away. Ken hurries away. Otto moves in his direction.

Cut to:

55. Exterior. Courtroom. Day.

People spill out down the steps, Ken among them. Otto falls in beside him.

OTTO. Hi, hon. How're you doing?

Ken starts but keeps moving. Otto stays with him.

Ooh, you look great. I love your hair. Do you have time for a coffee?

Ken declines, vigorously shaking his head.

KEN. Nnnn . . . I've gggot to gggg . . .

OTTO. Have you thought about it? One thing though . . . why did he give you this?

Otto has stopped. He has George's piece of paper in his hand. He reads aloud.

Eileen Coady, 69 Basil Street.

Ken's eyes pop. He grabs at his pocket, realizes and dashes to Otto.

What's he want you to do? Send her flowers? Do her shopping?

Ken tries to grab the paper back.

Show her a good time?
Rub her out? have a bit of noo . . .

Ken reacts to this. Otto stares at him. Ken looks furtive.

He wants you to rub her out?!

KEN (*suddenly nonchalantly*). Nnnn . . .

OTTO (*shouting to passers-by*). He's going to kill her, ah ha ha ha!

Ken makes a panicky move to hush Otto. The passers-by, punks, gawp.

OTTO (*to punks*). Fuck off or I'll kill you. You limey fruits.

The passers-by disappear.

So . . . the old lady's going to mmmmeet with an accident, eh, Kkkkkken?

Otto is laughing.

KEN. Ssshh . . . Ssshh! (*suddenly angry*) What's so funny?!

OTTO. Nothing, it's just that wasting old ladies isn't nice . . .

KEN. Well, it's bbbetter than bbbuggering people.

Otto is helpless with mirth. Ken gets the paper back. Otto controls himself.

OTTO. I bet you a pound you don't kill her.

KEN (*deeply, deeply angry*). . . . All right.

His jaw set, Ken stalks off. Otto calls after him, attracting attention.

OTTO. I love watching your ass when you walk. Is that beautiful or what? (*Shouting to passers-by*) Don't go near him, he's *mine*! A pound says you won't kill her.

Otto collapses into laughter once more.

We cut to Archie coming out of the courtroom in conversation with a legal friend, Zebedee. Wanda, in disguise, stands near enough to listen in.

ZEBEDEE. So when could you look at it?

ARCHIE. Well, let's think. Thursday's hopeless . . . I'll tell you what, my wife's going to the opera Friday evening, I could have a look at it then, and give you a call at the office Saturday morning.

ZEBEDEE. I'd really appreciate that. Thanks, Archie. Bye.

ARCHIE. Bye.

Wanda moves to Archie.

WANDA. Hi. I know we're not allowed to talk. Give me a call.

She slips a note into his breast pocket. Archie double-takes on Wanda's semi-disguise.

ARCHIE. I can't.

WANDA. Please?

ARCHIE. We're not allowed to speak.

WANDA. We don't have to. I don't want you for your conversation.

ARCHIE (*looking distressed*). I'd love to but . . .

Wanda's mouth starts to tremble and she breaks into loud sobs as she walks away. Archie doesn't know where to look.

Otto appears as Archie stares after her.

OTTO. What happened.

WANDA. Got a date Friday.

Cut to:

56. Interior. Laundry room. Mrs Coady's flat. Day.

Close-up of Ken, dressed in gasman's uniform. He reads the meter and, whistling loudly, glances into the corridor. It's empty. He suddenly grabs a pair of large, pink knickers from a pile, and stuffs them inside his shirt, still whistling. Mrs Coady appears.

MRS COADY. Look here, do you mind not making that terrible noise. My dogs will be having their nap.

Ken leans down to one of Mrs Coady's doglets.

KEN. Nice doggie, nice doggie.

The dog bites him. Ken shakes his hand in pain.

Cut to:

57. Exterior. Mrs Coady's block. Day.

Ken emerges, sucking his hand, and mounts his motorcycle.

Cut to:

58. Interior. Otto's car. Day.

Otto is in full lotus position in the driver's seat, meditating. Wanda gets in.

WANDA. Otto, what are you doing?

OTTO. It's a Buddhist meditation technique. (*he opens his eyes and unwraps his legs*) It focuses your aggression. The monks used to do it before they went into battle. (*he starts the engine*)

WANDA. . . . What kind of Buddhism is this, Otto?

Cut to:

59. Exterior. Street outside George's block. Day.

Otto drives off suddenly, causing a car to brake noisily. Otto hits his horn. We hear another crash.

Cut to:

60. Interior. Otto's car. Day.

OTTO. Asshole! It's an early Tantric meditation. (*he looks at Wanda's low-cut dress*) What is this?

WANDA. In order to get information. I just might have to get friendly with him.

Cut to:

61. Interior. Archie's house. Day.

Archie is mounting the stairs, carrying a brief. Wendy appears below dressed to go out. Portia lurks unenthusiastically.

WENDY. Well, we're ready now at last.

ARCHIE. Oh, good! Well . . . enjoy the opera, darling.

WENDY. Your supper's in the fridge, Archie.

ARCHIE. Oh, marvellous! Thanks so much.

WENDY. Be good.

Archie reacts.

Cut to:

62. Interior. Otto's car. Day.

OTTO. When you say 'friendly' . . . what are we talking about here? Cordial? Courteous? Supportive? What?

WANDA. I don't know. Let's just see what happens.

OTTO. So . . . friendly might include actual what? Penetration?

WANDA. Look! I don't need your jealousy now.

OTTO. . . . Jealousy!?

WANDA. Yes!

OTTO. Hey, I'm merely curious. Me, jealous of that . . . fop?

Cut to:

63. Interior. Kitchen, Archie's house. Day.

Archie goes to the fridge. He takes out a plate, on which is a pork pie, a stick of celery, a few tired lettuce leaves and two apples. He sighs, puts the stick of celery back and closes the fridge door.

Cut to:

64. Interior. Otto's car. Day.

WANDA. What about my tits?

OTTO (*casually*). Does he get to handle 'em?

WANDA. Yes. That's my forecast. I'll stand by that.

OTTO. Nuzzling?

WANDA. I think twenty million dollars is worth a little nuzzling. Eighty per cent chance there.

OTTO (*meanly*). Sucking?

WANDA. I thought you weren't jealous.

OTTO. I'm not! I don't believe in jealousy. It's for the weak. One thing, though. Touch his dick and he's dead.

Cut to:

65. Exterior. Suburban road. Day.

Otto's car roars past. We stay on another car, stationary at the side of the road, with a puncture. Wendy examines it. Portia sits in the car.

WENDY (*sighs furiously*). I told your father to get the car serviced.

PORTIA (*pleased*). Aren't we going, then?

WENDY. Oh, do shut up, Portia.

Cut to:

66. Interior. Den. Archie's house. Night.

Archie sits on a sofa, nibbling a lettuce leaf and reading a brief.

Cut to:

67. Exterior. Driveway, Archie's house. Night.

Otto is opening the front door with some CIA device.

WANDA (*whispers*). Hurry up.

The door opens. Wanda slips inside. Otto closes the door again quietly.

Cut to:

68. Interior. Den. Archie's house. Night.

Archie sits on the sofa. Wanda, looking Wandaful, stands inside the door.

WANDA. Hi.

Archie jumps and spins round. He stares at Wanda.

Do you despise me?

ARCHIE. No, that's not a word that leaps to mind.

WANDA. Can I stay, then?

Archie melts.

ARCHIE. Of course. Look, Wanda . . .

WANDA. I know, your wife's coming back.

ARCHIE. No, no, it's not her, she'll be gone for hours. It's about what I said to you . . . it *is* all right for us to speak . . . provided that we don't discuss the case.

WANDA. Oh . . . (*walking towards him*) Oh, fine . . .

ARCHIE. It's just that if anyone saw us talking, they'd think . . .

WANDA. Oh, but they won't.

Pause. Wanda takes off her glasses and blinks.

ARCHIE. . . . . Sorry if I seem . . . pompous.

WANDA. Oh, you're the best, Archie.

They move to kiss but Wanda suddenly pulls back.

No, not yet . . . I'm thirsty.

ARCHIE. What shall I get you?

WANDA. Whisky.

ARCHIE. . . . . You are the sexiest, most beautiful girl I have ever seen in my entire life.

WANDA (*softly*). Get me my drink . . .

Cut to:

69. Exterior. Lawn, Archie's house. Night.

From the garden, Otto looks up at the window and sees Archie locked in a passionate embrace. Archie carries Wanda across the room and they disappear from Otto's sight. He is worried.

Cut to:

70. Interior. Den. Archie's house. Night.

Archie and Wanda are on the sofa kissing.

WANDA (*moaning*). Oh, Archie . . . mmmm . . . so . . . if George decides to change his plea, he'd tell you where the loot is first, wouldn't he?

ARCHIE. Hmm? (*pauses*) Oh, darling, we mustn't talk about the trial.

WANDA. I know . . . I just meant theoretically. Kiss me there.

She points to her cleavage. Archie obliges, moving her locket out of the way.

ARCHIE (*muffled*). Oh, theoretically . . . well, if the defendant wants to change his plea in his instructions to his legal representative, the normal procedure . . .

Cut to Otto standing in the doorway peering at them.

Wanda sees him and mouths 'fuck off'. Otto signals to her to cool it and then moves behind the door.

Archie is still mumbling into Wanda's cleavage about criminal procedure but raises his head, sensing Wanda's restlessness.

What's the matter? . . .

WANDA (*pushing his head back down*). Oh, it's wonderful, Archie.

Suddenly she moans loudly.

Oh! Oh, you're getting me so hot. I need something to drink.

He reaches for her whisky.

Er, something cold . . . maybe in the fridge?

ARCHIE. Champagne?

WANDA. Oh, my favourite.

Archie gets up.

ARCHIE. Don't go away.

He disappears downstairs. Wanda goes over to Otto, who is behind the door. Her locket falls to the floor by the sofa.

WANDA (*furious*). What are you doing in here?

OTTO. Relax.

WANDA. Get the fuck out of here, Otto.

OTTO. I heard moaning, I was worried.

WANDA. I was faking it, you stupid jerk.

OTTO. Don't ever call me stupid. And I'm not jealous.

WANDA. Then leave.

OTTO. OK.

He shoves Wanda backwards on to the sofa.

(*looking around*) Nice place.

He goes towards the door.

Don't touch his dick.

Wanda is wriggling around trying to get up off the sofa. Suddenly Otto rushes back into the room.

His wife! His wife!

In a flash they have both disappeared, Otto hiding behind the door. A moment, and Wendy and Portia come up the stairs.

WENDY (*to Portia*). Now, for goodness sake get off to bed.

Wendy walks in and goes straight to the drinks cabinet. Portia goes upstairs. Wendy pours herself a whisky.

Oh God, there isn't any ice.

Wanda is frozen behind the drinks-cabinet door. She manages to retrieve her black scarf from the chair beside the cabinet.
Cut to Archie bounding upstairs with a champagne bottle and two glasses

*on a tray. He enters the room. Wendy is sitting on the sofa with her
back turned. She is wearing the same colour dress as Wanda, and Archie
doesn't realize it's her for a moment.*

ARCHIE. Champagne!

Wendy turns. Archie sees her and screams.

WENDY. What's the matter?

Archie's eyes flicker round the room. Wendy eyes the tray.

What are you doing?

ARCHIE. Champagne, dear . . . to welcome you home. Let me
pour you a glass.

*He puts the tray down, checking the room for Wanda. He starts pouring.
Wendy watches him, puzzled.*

WENDY. Whose is the car?

ARCHIE. . . . The car?

WENDY. Blocking the drive.

Archie's pouring get worse. He's filled two glasses.

ARCHIE. Ah, there you are, dear. Cheers! Well, nice to see you
again.

He drinks.

How was the opera, then? It finished early, did it . . .?

WENDY. Whose car is it?

Wanda, behind the cabinet door, realizes her locket is missing.

Otto appears from nowhere.

OTTO. Mine. It's a beauty, isn't it. Where did I leave my drink,
Archie?

Archie does not believe this is happening.

Ah!

He goes and picks up Wanda's glass.

WENDY (*quietly*). Who is this?

ARCHIE (*quietly*). . . . Don't you know?

OTTO (*to Wendy*). Hi. How d'you do, Mrs Leach. I'm Harvey Manfredjinsin . . . jen . . . I'm with the CIA.

WENDY. . . . CIA?

OTTO. That's correct, ma'am. I was just telling your husband here before I er . . . had to go to your beautiful bathroom . . . We've got a high-ranking KGB defector in a safe house near here . . . We're debriefing him as of now and we're just er . . . checking all the houses in the neighbourhood.

Archie is staring into space . . .

WENDY. For what?

OTTO. For KGB.

WENDY (*slightly irritated*). Is there any danger?

OTTO. No, no. Not now. We er . . . we er . . . just wanted to keep everyone informed. So, Archie, thanks for the drink. Sorry to have troubled you folks. I'll see myself out.

Otto makes to move off but Wendy puts a hand on his arm.

WENDY. Keep everyone informed . . .?

OTTO. So there's no panic, ma'am.

WENDY. But isn't it secret?

OTTO. You have no idea how secret.

WENDY. Well, why are you telling everyone?

OTTO. . . . It's a smokescreen?

WENDY. . . . *What?*

OTTO. Double bluff. Look, you obviously don't know anything about intelligence work, lady. It's an XK Red 27 technique.

WENDY. My father was in the Secret Service, Mr Manfredjinsinjen, and I know perfectly well that you don't keep the general public informed when you're debriefing KGB defectors in a safe house.

OTTO. Oh, you don't, huh?

WENDY. Not unless you're congenitally insane or irretrievably stupid, no.

OTTO. Don't call me stupid . . .

WENDY. Why on earth not?

Otto glowers, boiling.

OTTO. Oh, you English are *so* superior, aren't you? Well, would you like to know where you'd be without us, the old US of A, to protect you? I'll tell you – the smallest fucking province in the Russian Empire, that's what! So don't call me stupid, lady. Just thank me.

He turns and starts to leave. Wendy follows.

WENDY. Well, thank you for popping in and protecting us.

He leaves the room and goes downstairs. Wendy follows him out.

OTTO. . . . . If it wasn't for us, you'd all be speaking German, singing 'Deutschland Deutschland, Uber Alles' . . .

Meanwhile, Wanda appears from behind the door. Archie sees her.

WANDA. That's my brother. He is covering for me. Get rid of your wife and get my necklace.

ARCHIE. Necklace, right, right. I'll think of something to get rid of her.

Portia comes into the room.

PORTIA. Who are you talking to?

ARCHIE. Myself, darling.

PORTIA. Well, who was that shouting?

ARCHIE. The brother of a . . . of a friend of mine.

Wendy comes back into the room.

WENDY. Archie, who on earth . . .

ARCHIE. I don't know, extraordinary, he rang the bell and I opened the door and . . .

Wendy is heading for the drinks cabinet. Archie intercepts her.

Let's go to the pub.

WENDY. . . . What?

ARCHIE. Let's go to the pub. Get a drink there. Would you like to come, Portia?

Portia, sitting on the sofa, nods enthusiastically.

WENDY. We haven't been to the pub for fifteen years.

ARCHIE. No, well . . . be rather nice for Portia to see it now, wouldn't it, darling?

WENDY. Honestly, Archie.

Wendy closes the drinks-cabinet door. Archie screams, but Wanda has disappeared.

WENDY. What on earth is the matter?

ARCHIE. I thought . . . I thought the picture was falling off the wall.

WENDY. Will you pull yourself together.

ARCHIE. No, it's all right, it's quite secure.

Wanda is behind the sofa. She sees her locket on the floor and reaches out to get it, but Portia sees it first and picks it up.

PORTIA. What's this?

Archie realizes and moves fast.

ARCHIE (*snatching it*). Oh yes. Thanks, Portia. Well done. OK. Coming with us?

WENDY. What was that?

PORTIA. A kind of necklace.

Archie sees Wanda by the sofa and gasps.

WENDY. What's going on?

ARCHIE. Nothing dear. Right, let's go.

WENDY. Can I see that?

ARCHIE. What?

WENDY. In your hand.

Archie proffers an empty left hand.

Your other hand.

Archie, having switched the necklace behind his back, proffers an empty right hand.

Wendy takes his other hand, opens it and takes the locket.

ARCHIE. Portia, go to your room.

PORTIA. Aren't we going to the pub?

ARCHIE. Darling, I can explain everything. I left some papers at the office (*to Portia*) Now! (*to Wendy*) And they sent a new girl over . . .

WENDY. Oh, Archie!

ARCHIE. No really, she's Canadian, and she mentioned it was her birthday . . . so we . . .

WENDY. It's lovely. Thank you.

Wendy kisses him. Archie is stunned.

Oh, look, it's even got a W for Wendy.

ARCHIE. Oh, I'm so glad you like it, darling.

WENDY. It's the most beautiful thing you've ever given me.

She kisses Archie again. Archie suddenly grabs her and kisses her passionately, waving Wanda out of the room. He holds Wendy very tightly.

Archie . . . this isn't like you.

Wendy responds. The embrace intensifies. Wanda slips from her hiding place and out of the door. Archie watches her go with an agonized expression.

Cut to:

71. Exterior. Archie's house. Night.

Wanda comes out of the house and sees Otto.

WANDA (*whispering furiously*). Are you fucking crazy?

OTTO. Hey, I saved your ass.

WANDA. I had him right where I wanted him, you asshole. I give you one thing to do, Otto, one fucking thing – you're supposed to drive me here and shut up.

They disappear into the night, Wanda still berating Otto.

OTTO. Oh, relax!

Cut to.

72. Interior. Dining-room. Archie's house. Day.

The Leaches are finishing breakfast. Wendy is reading the paper, looking very relaxed. Archie, preoccupied, is trying to concentrate on a brief. The telephone rings. Portia runs in and picks it up eagerly.

PORTIA. Hallo? (*disgruntled*) Hold on. (*to Archie*) It's for you.

She leaves, dumping the phone. Archie picks it up.

ARCHIE. Hallo . . . Not at the moment, no . . yes, well, I'm not quite sure when I'll be able to get hold of that. (*he glances at Wendy's locket*) Yes. Yes, I do appreciate that. Yes, as soon as possible.

Wendy glances at him, sees him looking at her and happily indicates the locket. Archie beams uneasily.

ARCHIE. Well, that would be very nice, obviously. So . . . see you soon, I hope. Bye, Frank.

Cut to:

73. Exterior. Mrs Coady's block of flats. Day.

A slightly dirty yellow van with minimal windows is parked about thirty yards from the entrance to the block.

Inside the van are Ken and a huge, fearsome dog called Maggie. The dog is half Dobermann Pincher and half dragon. It is growling fearsomely. It has a muzzle on. Ken tries to keep it calm.

KEN. Easy, easy, Mmmmmmaggie. Easy, ggggirl. Easy.

Through the small window in the back, Ken sees Mrs Coady and her three little yapping dogs coming out of the block.

Here! Smell, smell!
Ken produces the stolen underwear and holds it to Maggie's muzzle. Maggie gets more excited.

Now, kkkkkill, kkkkkill.

He slips Maggie's muzzle off. Unfortunately, Maggie starts killing Ken.

From outside the van, which is rocking violently, we hear the sound of ferocious growling. Suddenly the doors burst open and Maggie leaps out on to the street, knickers around her head. She tosses them off and sniffs. She looks in the direction of Mrs Coady and sets off towards her at a terrifying lope. Ken appears at the back window of the van, covered in cuts, and stares after Maggie. Mrs Coady hardly sees Maggie before she is upon her. In one deft movement, Maggie takes one of the small dogs in her jaws and disappears down the street with it. Mrs Coady puts her hand to her heart. Ken looks distraught. Mrs Coady swallows a handful of pills.

Cut to.

74. Exterior. Kensington Pet Cemetery. Day.

Some earth is being thrown over a tiny grave covered with flowers. We close on Mrs Coady beside the grave. She is dressed in mourning clothes. Behind her are two choir boys.

VICAR. We therefore commit its body to the ground. Earth to earth, ashes to ashes, dust to dust. In sure and certain hope of the resurrection to eternal life.

The choir boys start to sing 'Miserere Dominum, Canis mortuus est'. Cut to Ken who is watching from behind a tree in the graveyard. He is a pitiful sight and is obviously in great distress. One arm is in a sling. A tear rolls down his cheek.

Cut to:

75. Interior. George's flat. Day.

Close on Otto knocking on the door. The door opens, revealing a bandaged Ken with a black armband.

OTTO. Hallo, honey. (*seeing the bandages*) What happened?

KEN. Nnnothing. (*he retreats, trying to conceal the armband*)

OTTO. (*pointing to it*). What's that? *Not* Granny?

KEN. Not yet, nnn . . .

OTTO. Who's it for, then?

KEN. A fff . . .

OTTO. A fish . . . a Frenchman . . . a phone operator?

KEN. A fffriend.

OTTO. A four-legged one? (*laughs at his little joke*) Where's my sister?

KEN. She's in the bbb . . . lavatory.

Otto wanders towards the bedroom calling . . .

OTTO. Wanda?

Wanda emerges from the bathroom. She is in the middle of several beauty treatments. Her hair is wrapped in pieces of tinfoil and she has depilatory cream over her moustache.

WANDA (*quietly but slightly excited*). Anything?

OTTO. What? No . . .

Wanda goes back into the bathroom.

WANDA (*louder*). Why are you here?

OTTO. I'm here because I'm bored. Bored wandering round this Godawful city shoving George's ugly pic . . . (*he glances out towards the main room*) . . . talking to a lot of snotty, stuck-up, intellectually inferior British faggots. Jesus, they're uptight.

He sees Wanda's handbag and starts poking around in it. He sees an envelope addressed 'Miss W Gershwitz' 'Private and Confidential'. He glances at the bathroom and sneaks the letter out.

They get rigor mortis in the prime of life in this country, standing there with their hair clenched, just counting the seconds till the weekend so that they can all dress up like ballerinas and . . .

Unfolding it, he starts as he sees something in the letter.

INSERT: 'See you at the flat at four. 2B St Trevor's Wharf, E1.'

. . . whip themselves into a frenzy at the flat at four, 2B Saint . . . (*checks himself*) to be honest I er . . . hate them . . . I mean (*he shoves the note back in the envelope*) pretending they're so fucking lawyer . . . er . . . *superior* . . . (*he puts the envelope in the bag*) so fucking superior with those phoney accents. (*he sees Ken at the door*) Not you, Ken, you've got a beautiful speaking voice . . . when it works.

Ken disappears, embarrassed. Otto gets up, takes a quick sniff of his armpit for courage.

(*to himself*) Sonofabitch!

He goes into the bathroom.

(*loudly*) So, want to have some lunch? (*quietly*) Have you heard from him?

WANDA (*quietly*). Who?

OTTO (*quietly*). Archie.

WANDA (*louder*). No, I have to finish my hair. (*quietly*) No . . .

OTTO (*quietly*). Nothing? (*loudly*) OK. Well, I'm outa here. (*quietly*) No plans to see him?

WANDA (*quietly*). No. (*louder*) OK. Bye, bro.

Otto wanders out of the bedroom.

OTTO. Bye, Wanda.

He picks up a photo of her and puts his fist through it, then hands it to Ken.

Oh! Sorry . . .

Ken stares at him as he exits.

Cut to:

76. Interior. Living-room. Archie's house. Day.

WENDY. What?!

ARCHIE. Well, it wasn't theirs to sell. You see, an old woman gave it to them to be engraved, she's about eighty and dying and it's of great sentimental value and somebody put it in the display cabinet by accident. So . . .

WENDY. That's their problem.

ARCHIE. Well, not really, darling, because legally they can't give title to it if . . .

WENDY. You paid for it.

ARCHIE. Yes, well, they do accept their mistake, darling, and that's why they're offering you this to replace it . . . (*producing a stunning pendant*) . . . You see, it's over three times as valuable and . . .

WENDY (*putting a hand on the locket which she's wearing*). This is the nicest thing you've ever given me, which I absolutely love, and now you want me to give it back and replace it with something awfully vulgar.

ARCHIE. I don't want you to give it back, darling . . .

WENDY. Well, they can't have it.

ARCHIE. Wendy.

WENDY. No.

ARCHIE. Wendy!!

WENDY. No. Tell them they can't have it. You're the bloody barrister.

She runs into the garden. Archie fumes impotently.

Cut to:

77. Exterior. Friend's flat. Day.

Wanda walks along a walkway above the river, looking at the numbers of the flats. She finishes munching a sandwich, throwing the remainder in the river, and checks the number on Archie's letter.

   Cut to:

78. Interior. Friend's flat. Day.

Archie checks his appearance in the mirror.

   Cut to:

79. Interior. Corridor outside friend's flat. Day.

Wanda is outside the door of the flat checking her appearance. She takes some scent out of her handbag, squirts it up her skirt, in her mouth, then smoothes down her dress. A deep breath. She rings the doorbell.

   Cut to:

80. Interior. Friend's flat. Day.

Archie opens the door.

WANDA. Hallo.

ARCHIE. Hallo.

   Wanda enters.

WANDA (*looking around*). Oh, Archie, it's beautiful. It's just beautiful.

   She walks through the flat to the balcony overlooking the river.

   Oh my God. Look! (*looking out over the water*) Oh, Archie, it's beautiful.

ARCHIE. Isn't it wonderful.

WANDA. Whose is it?

ARCHIE. It belongs to someone at the chambers.

WANDA. And where are they?

ARCHIE. Hong Kong.

WANDA. Ah so . . .

ARCHIE. Gone for weeks.

They go back inside.

WANDA. Nice rug, Archie.

She admires a thick white rug by the fireplace. Archie suddenly takes her hand.

ARCHIE. May I?

He polkas with her, flamboyantly if maladroitly, for a few seconds. Wanda is surprised.

WANDA. Archie, what are you doing?

ARCHIE. The polka, I think.

They slow down. Archie takes her in his arms.

You make me feel so free!

WANDA. . . . Free?

ARCHIE. Wanda, do you have any idea what it's like being English? Being so correct all the time, being so stifled by this dread of doing the wrong thing, of saying to someone 'Are you married?' and hearing 'My wife left me this morning', or saying 'Do you have children?' and being told 'They all burned to death on Wednesday.' You see, Wanda, we're all terrified of *embarrassment*. That's why we're so . . . *dead*. Most of my friends are dead, you know. We have these piles of corpses to dinner. But you're alive, God bless you. And I want to be. I'm so fed up with all this . . . I want to make love with you, Wanda. I'm a good lover. At least I used to be, back in the early fourteenth century. Can we go to bed?

WANDA (*kisses him*). Yeah.

She leaps to put her legs round his waist, and in this fashion he carries her up the stairs to the bedroom.

ARCHIE. Hang on!

They collapse on to the bed.

I think I love you, Wanda.

He opens her cardigan and puts his hand on her breast.

WANDA. Oh, Archie. Can I ask you a question?

Through the window right behind the bed, we see Otto, peering through.

ARCHIE. Anything.

WANDA. Where's my locket?

ARCHIE. I couldn't get it.

WANDA. What?!

Otto is trying to make out what they're saying.

ARCHIE. Well, Wendy wouldn't give it back. *Look* (*producing the new pendant*), I got you this instead . . . like it?

WANDA. No, Archie, I have to have mine.

She sits up and starts buttoning up her cardigan.

ARCHIE. What's the matter? Why?

WANDA (*choking*). My mother gave it to me. On her d . . . death . . . bed (*she leans against Archie, sobbing*).

Otto is very frustrated. He has a stethoscope to the glass but he still can't hear.

ARCHIE. All right, darling. I'll get it for you.

WANDA. You promise?

ARCHIE. I'll think of something.

Otto can't hear a thing, and gives up, taking another stimulating sniff of the armpit.

WANDA. Sex is very, very difficult for me with somebody that I don't trust completely.

ARCHIE. I promise I'll get it, OK?

WANDA (*suddenly bright again*). Oh, I love you, Archie. (*kisses him*) I've loved you ever since the first second I saw you.

Otto's head appears in the stairway beside the bed, trying to get to a better listening position. He reacts to this declaration and makes a noise. Archie hears it. His head comes up.

ARCHIE. What was that?

WANDA. What?

ARCHIE. Your brother didn't bring you here this time, did he?

WANDA. No! (*she laughs*)

ARCHIE. He's no idea?

WANDA. He doesn't have a clue.

ARCHIE. . . . What?

WANDA. He's so dumb.

ARCHIE. Really?

WANDA. He thought that the Gettysburg address was where Lincoln lived.

Otto looks slightly puzzled. Isn't it?

ARCHIE (*snorts with laughter*). All those terrible lies he told about the CIA! So painful . . .

WANDA. And when he heard your daughter's name was Portia, he said, 'Why did they name her after a car?'

They both howl with laughter. Wanda watches Archie with curiosity.

I love the way you laugh.

There is a moment between them.

ARCHIE. And I love you. You're funny. How come a girl as . . . bright as you, can have a brother, who's so . . .

Otto's head appears over the side of the bed, about two feet from them.

OTTO. Don't call me stupid.

They both see Otto and scream. They leap away from him across the bed.

ARCHIE. Jesus Christ!

WANDA. Otto!

In a flash, Otto has thrown Archie to the floor, grabbed Wanda by the wrist and is pulling her down the stairs by the neck.

OTTO. Come on.

WANDA. Otto! Ouch!

Otto shoves her out of the door of the flat into the corridor.

OTTO. I'll deal with you later.

He slams the door on her and turns. Archie has reached the bottom of the stairs. Wanda is hammering on the door.

ARCHIE. What have you done with her?

OTTO. She's all right. Now apologize.

WANDA (OOV). Otto!

ARCHIE. . . . What!!?

OTTO. Apologize!

WANDA (OOV). Shit.

ARCHIE. . . . Are you totally deranged?

OTTO. You pompous stuck-up snot-nosed English giant twerp scumbag fuckface dickhead asshole.

ARCHIE. How very interesting. You're a true vulgarian, aren't you?

OTTO. You're the vulgarian, you fuck. Now apologize.

ARCHIE. What . . . *me* to *you*?

OTTO. Apologize.

Cut to:

81. Exterior. Friend's flat. Day.

Close on Archie.

ARCHIE. All right. All right. I apologize . . .

OTTO (OOV). You're *really* sorry.

ARCHIE. I'm really, really sorry. I apologize unreservedly.

OTTO. You take it back . . .

The camera is turning through 180 degrees and now pulls back rapidly, to reveal Archie dangling upside down out of the window of the flat. Otto is holding him by his ankles. The river bed, uncovered by water at low tide, is seventy feet below.

ARCHIE. I do. I offer a complete and utter retraction. The imputation was totally without basis in fact, and was in no way 'fair comment' and was motivated purely by malice and I deeply regret any distress that my comments may have caused you or your family . . .

People on the bank below are staring up.

. . . And I hereby undertake not to repeat any such slander at any time in the future.

OTTO (*hesitates*). OK.

Cut to:

82. Exterior. Road outside Mrs Coady's block. Day.

The road is deserted. A scruffy yellow van waits, revving its engine.

Mrs Coady appears with her two remaining dogs, yapping noisily, from the entrance to block and turns away from the van. The van moves slowly off after her. Close on Ken as rasta, concentrating very hard.

Mrs Coady walks a few paces and reaches a zebra crossing. She steps out on to the crossing and one of her dogs starts pulling her across the road. The van accelerates. But the second dog tangles its leash round a lamp post and hauls Mrs Coady back on to the pavement.

Close on Ken as rasta, horrified. He swings the wheel to avoid the dog in the road.

The van swerves across the road, hits a council rubbish bin and crashes to a halt. We close on the zebra crossing where there lies a very flat dog indeed. Mrs Coady, realizing what's happened, staggers backwards and sits down on the pavement, gasping for air. Ken gets out of the mangled van and for a moment just stares, mortified, at the squashed animal. Then he panics and runs away up the street, throwing off his rasta disguise as he goes.

Cut to:

83. Exterior. Kensington Pet Cemetery. Day.

'Miserere Dominum, Miserere Dominum, canis mortuus est.' As Mrs Coady, the Vicar and the two choirboys make their way out of the graveyard, we close on Ken laying down some flowers beside a tiny grave, marked 'Lucky'. Tears are pouring down his cheeks. He has a bandage round his head and a patch over one eye. He wipes the tears away from his good eye.

Cut to:

84. Exterior. Friend's flat. Day.

A row is in progress. Wanda and Otto, two distant figures, approach.

OTTO. You said you loved him!

WANDA (*shouting furiously*). That's right, Otto. Now here's a multiple choice question for you. a) Wanda was lying. b) Wanda was telling the truth . . . Which one are you going to pick?

OTTO. What was the first one? . . . You told me you were not planning to see him.

WANDA (*storming ahead*). Because I knew you'd come along and fuck it up. I was dealing with something delicate, Otto. I'm setting up a guy who's incredibly important to us, who's going to tell me where the loot is and if they're going to come and arrest you, and you come loping in, like Rambo without a jockstrap, and you dangle him out of a fifth-floor window. Now was that smart? . . . Was it shrewd? . . . Was it good tactics? . . . Or was it . . . STUPID!?

OTTO (*stopping*). Don't call me stupid.

WANDA (*turns*). Oh, right. To call you stupid would be an insult to stupid people. I've known sheep that could outwit you. I've worn dresses with higher IQs. But you think you're an intellectual, don't you, ape?

OTTO. Apes don't read philosophy.

WANDA. Yes they do, Otto. They just don't understand it. Now let me correct you on a couple of things, OK? Aristotle was not

Belgian. The central message of Buddhism is not 'Every Man For Himself'.

OTTO. You read . . .

WANDA. And . . . the London Underground is not a political movement. Those are all mistakes, Otto, I looked them up.

Otto, for once, is deflated. Wanda sits down on a wall beside the river.

Now . . . You have just (*putting her arm around him as if he were a miscreant child*) assaulted the one man who can keep you out of jail and make you rich. So what are you going to do about it, huh? What would an intellectual do? What would Plato do?

OTTO (*quietly*). . . . Apologize.

WANDA. Pardon me.

OTTO (*still mumbling*). Apologize.

WANDA. What?

OTTO (*louder, defiantly*). Apologize!!

WANDA. Right. (*she rises*)

OTTO. . . . I'm sorry.

WANDA. No. Not to me. To Archie. And make it good . . . or we're dead.

Cut to:

85. Exterior. Archie's house. Day.

Otto's car pulls up in the road outside the house. Otto is rehearsing.

OTTO. Oh, I'm so very very very very s . . . *fuck you.*

He gets out of the car and walks into the driveway.

I'm very s . . . very very very s . . .

He looks at his watch and sits down in the middle of the drive in a lotus position.

I'm very s . . . very very . . .

Suddenly there is the sound of glass breaking. Otto looks round, rolls over backwards and leaps to his feet.

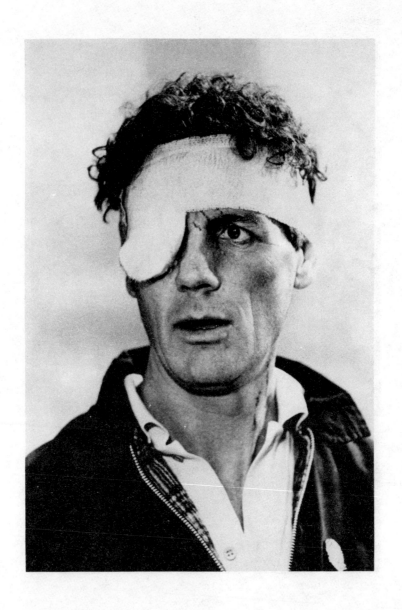

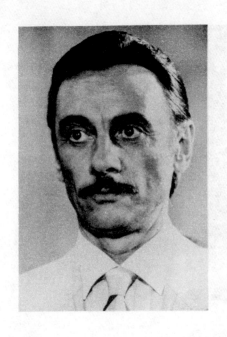

Cut to:

86. Interior. Ground floor. Archie's house. Day.

A man's black-gloved hand is opening the back door from the outside, through a broken pane. He enters, and hurries through the hall and upstairs. Otto reaches the window and peers in.

Cut to:

87. Interior. Bedroom, Archie's house. Day.

The intruder enters and opens Wendy's jewellery drawer. He takes the locket and a few other pieces, puts them into a bag and tips a couple of drawers out on to the floor. We see that the burglar is Archie.

Cut to:

88. Interior. Ground floor. Archie's house. Day.

Otto comes through the back door into the hall. We hear loud crashing sounds from upstairs.

Cut to:

89. Interior. Bedroom, Archie's house. Day.

Archie is making it look convincing. He empties several drawers of clothes on to the floor and then hurries downstairs.

Cut to:

90. Ground floor. Archie's house. Day.

Archie heads into the living-room. Otto follows and sees the back of Archie, who is rummaging through a cupboard, emptying the contents on to the floor. Archie picks an ornament off the mantelpiece and drops it deliberately. It smashes into hundreds of pieces. He raises his fist triumphantly and runs out into the hall. Almost immediately he comes spinning back in, with a raincoat over his head and his arms pinned to his sides, followed by Otto. Archie falls over a small table.

OTTO. Hallo, Mr Burglar. Going somewhere? Thought you could rob Mr Leach, eh? Well, I'm going to teach you a lesson. He just happens to be a very good friend of mine . . .

Otto kicks Archie, who staggers round the room, bent double.

. . . and he's going to be very pleased with me, when he finds you . . .

ARCHIE (*muffled*). No! Otto!

Otto reaches a large copper warming pan down off the wall, as Archie, making muffled noises, tries to stand up.

OTTO. . . . all tied up and ready for the police.

ARCHIE (*muffled*). Otto. No! Otto . . . Otto . . .

Otto brings the pan down on Archie's head with an awful bong.

OTTO. And don't call me Otto. To you I'm Mr . . .

He stops. Archie slumps unconscious. Otto has disturbing thoughts. He drops to the floor and pulls the raincoat off Archie's head. He stares. And panics.

. . . Aaaagh! Oh my God!! (*dropping to his knees*) I'm sorry. I'm sorry. I'm sorry. Please, I'm sorry. I didn't know it was you! (*stroking Archie's cheek to see if he is still alive*) How could I know it was you? How could you expect me to guess? (*he gets up*) Stupid jerk, I mean, what the fuck are you doing robbing your own house? You asshole!

He starts kicking Archie.

You stupid stiff pompous English . . . aagh!

He stops, horrified.

Oh, I'm sorry, I'm sorry . . . Er . . .

He ponders deeply and runs for it.

Cut to:

91. Exterior. Archie's house. Day.

Bang! Wendy slams the door of her car in the drive. She walks to the back door. Otto emerges from the front door, unseen by her, and hurries away.

Cut to:

92. Interior. Living-room. Archie's house. Day.

Archie stirs and opens his eyes. He suddenly comes to, and discovers his hands are tied. Then he hears Wendy coming through the front door and reacts with horror. But Wendy goes upstairs. Archie sees the bag. He stares. From upstairs comes a scream.

WENDY (OOV). God almighty! Bloody hell!

Archie picks the bag up with his teeth and scatters the contents. Wendy is running down the stairs. Archie sees the locket and somehow gets it and the chain in his mouth and slumps, feigning unconsciousness, just as Wendy bursts in. She sees him, cries and runs to him. Archie feigns waking up, making moaning noises. Wendy kneels by him.

WENDY. Darling, are you hurt? Speak to me.

Archie groans.

Are you hurt?

Archie merely moans.

Can't you speak?

Archie groans sympathetically and indicates his tied hands. Wendy starts untying him.

Archie! Archie! What has happened?

Archie, hands free, stages a coughing fit and gets the locket into his hand and then his pocket.

Archie, we've been burgled.

ARCHIE. Oh *no*!

WENDY. Well, are you hurt?

ARCHIE. No, no, I'm fine. Bit of a headache. I came in here, somebody hit me, tied me up with a . . .

Suddenly he sees his watch and starts.

My God, is that the time!?

Wendy stares at him.

WENDY. . . . What?

ARCHIE. I didn't realize it was quite so late.

WENDY. What?!

He gets up. Wendy stares at him in astonishment.

ARCHIE. I'm late for a conference.

WENDY. . . . A *conference*!! You've just been *attacked* . . .!

ARCHIE. No, it's nothing, darling. Look I must fly, sorry.

WENDY. Archie . . .

ARCHIE. I'll help you tidy up when I get back.

Archie hurries out. Portia wanders in casually.

Oh, hallo, Portia.

PORTIA. What's happened?

The front door slams.

WENDY. Your father has finally gone completely mental.

Cut to:

93. Interior. Friend's flat. Day.

Archie bursts in, breathless, and hurries through to the kitchen clutching two bottles of champagne. He comes back into the living-room, checks his appearance in the mirror and looks at his watch.

Cut to:

94. Interior. Corridor outside friend's flat. Day.

Outside the door, Wanda prepares to ring. But this time she does so differently – quite demurely, by her standards. Then she reaches for the bell.

Cut to:

95. Interior. Friend's flat. Day.

Archie opens the door. Wanda steps in.

WANDA. Hi.

She leans forward and kisses Archie gently.

ARCHIE. Hi.

He gives her another kiss. Halfway through, Wanda's eyes register surprise. She pulls back from him and removes a locket which is half-protruding from her mouth. She looks at it, then at Archie and smiles.

WANDA. Archie. Thank you so much.

ARCHIE. Champagne?

WANDA. OK.

Archie makes for the kitchen. Wanda opens the locket, sees the key, breathes a sigh of relief and puts the locket on. Archie appears with two glasses. He gives her one.

To us.

ARCHIE. To us.

They toast and start to drink.

Well, I went back to the house and guess who . . .

Wanda has emptied her glass in three gulps. She tosses the glass behind her. It smashes in the fireplace.

WANDA. Let's make love.

Archie looks at her.

ARCHIE. Well, if you absolutely insist.

He takes her hand and takes a step towards the bedroom.

WANDA (*restraining him*). No.

ARCHIE. What?

WANDA. Here . . . on the rug.

She takes some sexy underwear out of her handbag and heads towards the stairs.

(*giving him a kiss*) I'll be right back. Get undressed.

ARCHIE. Why not? Why not, indeed.

He throws his glass into the fireplace. It smashes. He starts to undress, and calls to Wanda who is upstairs.

Afterwards . . .

WANDA. Yeah?

ARCHIE. Let's go to South America.

Wanda's face appears on the balcony level upstairs.

WANDA. What?

ARCHIE. Let's fly to South America.

WANDA. Why South America?

ARCHIE. OK. Iceland.

Wanda, more or less reassured, disappears. Archie takes his shirt off.

What do you really want out of life, Wanda?

WANDA (*taking off her shoes*). I don't know.

ARCHIE. Why do I like you so much?

WANDA. Archie?

ARCHIE. Hmm?

WANDA. Do you speak Italian?

ARCHIE. I am Italian. *Sono Italiano in spirito ma ho sposato una donna che preferisce laborare nel giardino a far l'amore passionata. Un sbaglio grande.*

Archie's accent is better than Otto's. Wanda is writhing on a chair upstairs in total ecstasy.

But it's such an ugly language. How about . . . Russian?

He unleashes a flow of superb Russian. Wanda falls to the floor, moaning and struggling to remain conscious, as a drop of saliva creeps downwards from the corner of her mouth. Her thighs caress the safety rope.

Archie cavorts round the room, maintaining the flow of luscious Russkie chat. Wanda, hardly undressed at all, looks over the edge of the balcony. She wipes the saliva with her hand.

WANDA. Archie?

He stops for a moment.

ARCHIE. Yes.

WANDA. Are you rich?

ARCHIE. No, no, I'm afraid not.

WANDA. What about the house?

ARCHIE. That's Wendy's. She's the rich one.

WANDA (*thoughtful*). Oh . . .

She disappears. Archie starts up the Russian again, removes first his socks, which he bounces off his arm, then his underpants, flicks them up with his foot and spins around Nureyev-style with his underpants on his head. The door of the flat opens and in walk the Johnson family — a couple in their forties, three children, thirteen, eight and six, a nanny and a baby. They are all through the door before they see Archie. They now all stare at each other for a very long time. The parents are so astonished they do little to restrain their children's natural curiosity.

Archie, mid-spin, suddenly sees them and freezes. He stands, open-mouthed, then, suddenly realizing he is completely naked, grabs a framed photograph of a smiling Mrs Johnson to conceal his private parts.

MR JOHNSON (*eventually finding his voice*). What the hell are you doing?

ARCHIE. I might ask you the same question.

MR JOHNSON. Who are you???

ARCHIE. What?

MR JOHNSON. Get your clothes on.

ARCHIE. Will you leave immediately please.

MR JOHNSON. What?!!!

ARCHIE. You're in the wrong flat. This flat belongs to Patrick Balfour, he's in Hong Kong, and he lent me the key. Now *get out!*

MR JOHNSON. But we leased it from the agents last weekend.

Archie takes a moment to digest this piece of information.

ARCHIE. Yes, well, that obviously changes things a bit. Umm . . .

MRS JOHNSON. Aren't you Archie Leach?

ARCHIE (*dying quietly*). What?

MRS JOHNSON. You bought our house in Lissenden Gardens . . . Hazel and Ian Johnson.

ARCHIE. . . . What a coincidence. How . . . nice to see you.

Cut to:

96. Exterior. Towpath by Kipling Mansions. Night.

Archie stands, staring at the water in deep suffering. He turns round and looks up at Wanda's bedroom window, then gets into his car and starts dialling on his car-phone.

Cut to:

97. Interior. George's flat. Night.

Wanda is lying on the bed, idly swinging the locket from her feet. The phone rings. She picks it up.

WANDA. Hallo?

ARCHIE (OOV). Hallo, Wanda? It's Archie.

Wanda smiles, obviously pleased he's rung.

Cut to:

98. Interior. Archie's car. Night.

ARCHIE. I can't see you any more. I've got to end it. I'm sorry.

Cut to:

99. Interior. George's flat. Night.

WANDA. What?

ARCHIE (OOV). I'm sorry.

The phone clicks.

WANDA. Archie?

No response. Wanda replaces the receiver slowly and stares blankly into the distance. She is very upset.

Cut to:

100. Exterior. Archie's house. Night.

Archie's car turns into the driveway and stops. Archie sits for a moment at the wheel, then wipes a tear from his eye. He gets out and turns as he hears a noise in the drive. It is Otto.

OTTO. OK.

ARCHIE. Oh no! No! Please!

Archie throws up his arms and backs away.

OTTO. Look, I want to apologize.

ARCHIE. I've just finished it, all right?

OTTO. OK, now wait . . . wait a moment.

Archie runs away. Otto gives chase, calling after Archie, as they run round the grounds. We hear them faintly . . .

ARCHIE. I just ended it for Christ's sake, will you leave me alone?

OTTO. Wait! Wait . . . I just want to say I'm sorry . . . wait . . .

ARCHIE. No! No! Please . . . I've ended it. I swear it.

Otto eventually catches up with Archie and forces him to the ground.

It's all over, OK?

OTTO. It's all right.

ARCHIE. Don't beat me up again, please. I've had a terrible day.

Otto pulls out a gun and sticks it against Archie's nose.

OTTO. Will you shut up.

ARCHIE. Oh, Jesus Christ, don't kill me, please.

OTTO. Shut up then. OK, look. I just want to apologize sincerely
. . . for . . . what . . . well, when I dangled you out of the
window, I'm really, really . . . well it was not a nice thing to do.
And then when I attacked you in there, well, I'm really really
s . . . how could I know you were trying to rob your own
house . . .

*A light goes on in the house. Wendy appears at the bedroom window,
which is open. She peers out, sees the two figures and listens.*

I was just trying to help.

Archie cannot move, the gun is still squashing his nose.

ARCHIE. Yes, thanks. Thanks, Otto.

OTTO. I wanted you to trust me.

ARCHIE. Please. It was my fault. It was my fault.

OTTO. That's true. Now, about my sister.

ARCHIE. Otto, I've just fin . . .

OTTO. She's a very sexy girl, I understand you wanting to play
around with her.

Wendy's face sets.

ARCHIE. Otto . . .

OTTO. It's OK, I was wrong. I'm sorry I was jealous. Just go
ahead, pork away, pal. Fuck her blue. I like you, Archie, I just
wanna help.

Upstairs, her face like thunder, Wendy closes the window and disappears.

Cut to:

101. Interior. House opposite Mrs Coady's block of flats. Day.

Ken is in position behind a telescopically sighted rifle. He looks through the sight with his good eye. It is lined up with Mrs Coady's front door.

The door opens. Ken peers down. Mrs Coady is emerging slowly. Ken moves the telescope's POV upwards until the cross wires are focused just above a large concrete block which is suspended from some scaffolding on the front of the building.

Mrs Coady moves out of the door towards the pavement, leading her remaining dog.

Ken watches her for a moment, and then returns to the sight. She steps down on to the pavement. Ken fires. The bullet hits a pulley. A pause. The rope through the pulley suddenly starts to feed through and the block descends. Mrs Coady checks for rain, as she always does. Hearing a thunderous roaring sound, she steps back on to the steps, pulling the dog back with her, to put her brolly up.

The stone block plummets on to the dog behind her. Ken screams. Mrs Coady gets the umbrella up and walks off. The leash tightens. She returns for her dog. But the leash terminates in a concrete block. She continues to look around for her dog.

KEN. Oh God!

Ken reels against the wall, making agonized noises.

Through the window we see a crowd of people gathering around the concrete block.

Cut to:

102. Exterior. Mrs Coady's block of flats. Day.

Ken comes out on to the pavement in a daze. By now there is a great commotion across the street. Ken walks across the road towards the crowd. He peers through the cluster and stares down at the body of Mrs Coady. A policeman pulls a blanket over her. Gradually Ken understands. A smile spreads across his face. He starts laughing maniacally. The crowd look at him astonished. He disappears, cackling.

Cut to:

103. Interior. Visiting-room. Jail. Day.

George is in mid-ecstatic-leap. He capers about a bit, watched by two warders and Ken, who grins insanely.

GEORGE. Unbe-fucking-lievable!

One of the warders starts towards him.

WARDER. Thomason!

George sits back down, trying to control himself.

GEORGE (*quietly*). You done well, my son. Now . . . here's the plan. Get four tickets for this evening for Rio, first class, then . . .

KEN. Ffff . . .?

GEORGE. Yes, four. We get rid of Otto later. Then . . . back to the flat, pack, collect me, then to the Cathcart Towers Hotel to pick up the jewels.

George looks at Ken and, unable to contain his delight any longer, gets up, hugs him and shouts:

Unbe-fucking-lievable!

WARDER. Oi! Oi!

Cut to:

104. Interior. George's flat. Day.

Wanda and Ken are dancing a rumba around the flat. Both are ecstatic.

WANDA. Oh, it's so great, I can't believe it.

KEN. He's ssssafe . . .

She gives him an extra hug and kiss, and looks at her watch.

WANDA. Oh, I'm gonna be late for court.

She picks up her bag. The phone goes. Ken goes to answer it.

KEN (*to phone*). Hallo? . . . Oh, hallo, Otto . . .

Wanda indicates she's not there, and leaves.

Ah, she just left. Oh . . . and Otto . . . you owe me a ppp . . .

Cut to:

105. Interior. George's flat. Day.

Otto bursts through the front door.

OTTO. What?!

Ken smiles smugly, and returns to his packing.

KEN. You owe me a pppound.

OTTO (*unbelieving*). . . . Not Granny.

KEN. Mmmmmet with an accident.

OTTO. Bullshit! You're lying!

KEN. Come on.

He holds his hand out for the money.

OTTO. . . . Dead??!

KEN. Heart attack . . .

OTTO. I don't believe this.

KEN. So Ggeorge'll be out this afternoon, we all go up to Heathrow, collect the loot and (*he mimes a plane flying off with appropriate noises*) All thanks to me.

Otto looks at him and slowly starts to smile.

OTTO. So the loot's at the airport, is it, Ken?

Ken's face falls.

Cut to:

106. Interior. Kitchen, George's flat. Day.

Ken is trussed up on a chair, near the fish tank. Otto sits at the breakfast bar eating a plate of chips. Ken looks up groggily.

KEN. Wwhat's happening?

OTTO. Well, Ken, I'm going to ask you some questions . . .

Ken looks apprehensive.

. . . while I eat my chips. First, who was the philosopher who developed the concept of the Superman in *Also Sprach Zarathustra*?

Ken looks suitably dumbstruck.

No?

Otto eats a chip, takes another and inserts it in Ken's nostril.

That's a chip up the nose, I'm afraid. Friedrich Nietzsche. Next. In which book did Nietzsche claim that almost all higher culture is based on cruelty?

Ken is open-mouthed.

Are you thinking, or are you in mid-stutter?

KEN. You're mmm . . . mad.

Ken gets a chip up the other nostril, with some ketchup on it.

OTTO. *Beyond Good and Evil.* Guess I'll have to ask you an easy one, huh, Ken? Er . . . OK. Let me think. (*sudden inspiration*) Where are the diamonds? I'll give you a clue. Somewhere around the airport.

Ken gets the point.

KEN. I'm nnn . . . nnn . . .

OTTO. No hassle, there's plenty of time, Ken. I'll just sit here and eat my chips till you tell me.

Otto eats one. Ken almost relaxes.

The English contribution to world cuisine. The chip.

Otto eats another.

What do the English usually eat with chips to make them more interesting? (*puts on BBC accent*) Wait a moment . . .

Otto's eyes slowly come round to the fish tank.

It's fish! Isn't it?

Otto goes over to the tank, picks up a little net and starts fishing. Ken stares with a Room 101 expression on his face. Otto catches a fish, lifts it out of the water and sniffs it appraisingly.

Here, boy. Down the hatch.

He swallows the fish. And smacks his lips. Ken is speechless.

Delicious.

KEN. You . . . bbbb . . .

OTTO. Better eat the green one? OK.

Otto gets a green one and shows it to Ken.

What's this one's name? Not Wanda, anyway.

Ken reacts.

I'm going to call her lunch. Hallo, lunch! Hallo.

Otto eats the green one. He makes a sour face.

Yeeuch. Avoid the green ones, they're not ripe yet.

Laughs at his joke. Ken is almost fainting.

Cut to:

107. Interior. Courtroom. Day.

A full, formal court is in session, well attended by the general public. Archie and Percival sit on the benches. George is in the dock, with two warders.

Archie rises to cross-question Inspector Marvin, who arrested George.

ARCHIE. Now you were in court, were you not, Inspector, when the forensic evidence was read?

INSPECTOR. . . . Yes, sir.

Wanda, dressed arrestingly in white, tries to gain admittance but an official turns her away. She sticks up her middle finger, the American equivalent of a V-sign.

ARCHIE. And the fact that Mr Thomason was installing windows the previous weekend would account, would it not, Inspector, for the presence of small particles of glass on his trousers?

The Inspector can't think of anything to say.

No hurry, Inspector . . . **Please do take your time.**

Cut to:

108. Interior. George's flat. Day.

Tears pour down Ken's face. The fishtank is almost devoid of fish. Otto swallows.

OTTO. I'm almost full. (*he looks at Wanda the fish*) Almost.

KEN. Stop!

Otto is interested.

Pppplease ddddon't eat Wwww . . .

Otto fishes Wanda out with the net.

OTTO. Come on, Wanda. Gullet time.

He catches her, and shows her, in the net, to Ken.

What are the names of those hotels that are right by the airport, Ken? What are they, the Airway Sheraton? The Post House? The Cathcart Towers?

Ken's face flickers.

The Cathcart Towers! Yes?

He pops Wanda in his mouth. Her tail protrudes.

(*indistinctly*). Hhmmm? Yes?

KEN (*after a terrible struggle*). Yes!

OTTO. In a safe-deposit box?

KEN. Yes!

OTTO. Where's the key?

Ken can't understand him.

KEN. Wwww . . .?

Otto spits Wanda out of his mouth.

OTTO (*clearer*). Where's the key?

Ken agonizes. Then:

KEN. In the ttttank.

Otto flies to the tank.

OTTO. Where?

Ken cannot speak. Otto puts Wanda back into his mouth.

KEN. In the tttt . . .

OTTO. . . .Treasure chest!!!

*Otto pulls the treasure chest out, opens it, and tips it out. It is empty.
He shows it to Ken. Ken is astounded.*

Where?

Ken, hopelessly, shrugs. Otto swallows. Ken screams.

KEN. Aaaagh. You . . . bbb . . . I'll kkkk . . .

*Otto looks at him, takes a pear from the fruit bowl and puts it into
Ken's mouth.*

OTTO. Sorry, Ken, but your answer was incorrect. Still, you really
did think it was in there, didn't you?

Strange sounds are coming from Ken, who is going purple.

What?

*Ken continues to suffocate until Otto removes the chips from his nose.
Ken takes in huge gasps of air.*

Cut to:

109. Interior. Lobby. Old Bailey. Day.

Wanda goes over to a payphone and picks up the receiver.

WANDA. Hallo?

Cut to:

110. Interior. George's flat. Day.

Otto is holding the receiver. Ken, demented, is in the background.

OTTO. I know where the diamonds are.

   Cut to:

111. Interior. Lobby. Old Bailey. Day.

Wanda thinks.

WANDA. Where?

   Cut to:

112. Interior. George's flat. Day.

OTTO. . . . Where's the key?

   Long pause.

   Cut to:

113. Interior. Lobby. Old Bailey. Day.

WANDA. I've got it.

   Cut to:

114. Interior. George's Flat. Day.

OTTO. How soon can you get to George's apartment?

   Cut to:

115. Interior. Courtroom. Day.

Archie is cross-examining Wanda in the witness box.

ARCHIE. You are Wanda Gershwitz of Kipling Mansions, Murray
   Road, London W9?

WANDA. Yes.

   George, in the defendant's stand, is looking smug.

ARCHIE. Now, will you tell the court please how do you know the defendant?

WANDA. We've had a relationship for two years.

JUDGE. Relationship?

WANDA. We're lovers, your lord.

ARCHIE. Miss Gershwitz, on the 4th of March of this year . . . in the morning, where were you?

WANDA. I was at the apartment at Murray Road.

ARCHIE. And were you by yourself or was there anyone else present?

WANDA. No. Somebody else was there.

ARCHIE. And who was that?

WANDA. My brother.

ARCHIE. And did your . . . (*he does a take*) Your *brother*?

WANDA (*repeating louder, as if he hadn't heard her*). My brother.

ARCHIE. Yes . . . and . . . are you quite sure it was your brother?

JUDGE. Mr Leach, I'm sure Miss Gershwitz can recognize her brother. She's had a relationship with him all her life.

Much laughter in the courtroom.

ARCHIE. Ha ha . . . much obliged, my lord. Ahm . . . was there anyone else present that morning?

WANDA. Yes, George was there.

ARCHIE. Thank you . . .

George relaxes, still puzzled.

WANDA. But he left about five to seven.

ARCHIE. . . . Wanda . . .

The Judge turns sharply to Archie. Archie realizes his mistake.

I wanda . . . I wonder . . .

George is starting to look frightened.

I wonder . . . I wonder . . .

Archie looks around the courtroom, wondering. He gazes up at the gallery and to his astonishment, sees Wendy sitting there. He goes totally blank. A long pause. George is ominously still.

JUDGE. . . . Yes, Mr Leach?

Archie tries to recover.

ARCHIE. I wendy, I wanda, I wonder . . . when you say five to seven, Miss Gershwitz . . . how can you be so sure?

WANDA. Oh, I looked at the clock, 'cos I was saying to myself, 'Where could he be going at five to seven with that sawn-off shotgun?'

ARCHIE. Darling!

Archie realizes and stares up at Wendy, who glares at him. The Judge is astonished.

JUDGE. Mr *Leach*! 'Darling'?!

Archie swings round to him.

ARCHIE. Yes, dear?

George suddenly moves. He vaults over the front of the dock and hurtles towards Wanda.

GEORGE. You bitch! You fucking bitch!

All hell breaks loose in court. George lunges towards the witness box and grabs Wanda, who screams.

JUDGE. Restrain that man!

Archie grabs George from behind, wrestling him away from Wanda. George elbows Archie in the groin, who reels back and lands. People pile on top of George. Wanda runs round the courtroom trying to escape. The Judge tries to restore order.

Restrain this man.

The Clerk of the Court starts shouting.

CLERK. Clear the court! Clear the court!

Eventually George is restrained by two police officers and the court is cleared. Archie lies on a bench, dazed.

Wendy comes into the courtroom. A policeman tries to stop her.

WENDY. Bloody hell! (*to policeman*) It's my husband. He's been hit.

She approaches Archie, who is rising unsteadily to his feet. He sees Wendy.

ARCHIE. Ah. You made it, good. Bit of a knock, I'm afraid.

He indicates his eye. Wendy slaps him right on the same spot. He staggers, and falls.

WENDY. I have never been so humiliated in my life. You can stick this marriage right in your bottom. I'll see you in court.

She storms out of the courtroom. Archie gets up. He has a strange, resigned look on his face.

ARCHIE. Yes . . . well . . . that's it, then.

He puts his wig back on.

Cut to:

116. Interior. Cell. Old Bailey. Day.

George is standing looking dishevelled. The two warders are with him. Archie walks in. George ignores him.

ARCHIE. George . . .

GEORGE. What?

ARCHIE. We've got to talk . . .

GEORGE. You tell those pigs to fuck off.

ARCHIE. Fuck off, pigs.

This causes real surprise among our bluebottle friends, who stare open-mouthed. Even George is half thrown.

Did you hear what I said? Fuck off.

The policemen leave.

What's she up to, George?

GEORGE. What are you up to? You called her darling. And Wanda.

ARCHIE. I've been helping her get her evidence straight, you berk. It slipped out.

GEORGE. . . . You been coaching her?

ARCHIE. What do you think? Look George, we've got ten minutes. They're going to find you guilty, right? Now, if you plead guilty now and tell them where the loot is, you may get away with eight years, out in five and a half.

GEORGE. What if I tell them about Otto? And Wanda?

ARCHIE. They both did it?

George nods.

Great. All right . . . maybe six years, out in four. So where are the diamonds?

GEORGE. Where's Bartlett?

ARCHIE. He's upstairs trying to calm things down. So, where are they?

GEORGE. Tell Bartlett Ken knows where they are.

ARCHIE. George, it'd be a lot quicker if you told me.

George looks at him scornfully.

OK. I'll tell Bartlett. Where's Ken?

GEORGE. He's at the flat.

Cut to:

117. Interior. Stairs between dock and cell. Day.

Archie is flying down them. He reaches the bottom and looks out into the foyer. He sees a distraught Wanda with the policeman and the usher by the washrooms.

WANDA (*sobbing*). Thank you for all your help. I'll be right out.

She disappears into the Ladies. Archie thinks.

Cut to:

118. Exterior. Old Bailey. Day.

Archie hurries down the steps of the Old Bailey and around the corner, just in time to see Wanda climbing over a wall on to the pavement. She hurries across the road and tries to hail a cab. The cab does not stop and Wanda goes in search of another. Archie catches up with her, takes her by the arm and hurries her away from the Old Bailey.

WANDA. Taxi. Taxi. Please. Shit.

ARCHIE. Come on.

WANDA (*startled*). What?!

ARCHIE. Let's go.

WANDA. Where?

ARCHIE. Buenos Aires . . .

WANDA. What?

Archie hurries with Wanda trotting beside him, along the relatively crowded pavement.

ARCHIE. We're going to George's flat first.

They reach Archie's car. Wanda stares.

Get in.

She gets in.

Archie symbolically chucks his robe and wig into a refuse bin. Then he gets into the car.

Got your passport?

WANDA. Yeah.

ARCHIE. Right. Check the briefcase for mine. Get your head down.

He drives off, past the Old Bailey.

Cut to:

119. Interior. Archie's car. Day.

ARCHIE. So . . . you robbed the jeweller's, turned one of your lovers over to the police, kept the other one on to help you find the diamonds and, when he does, you commit perjury in the High Court, right?

WANDA. Oh, come on, Archie, everybody does it in America.

ARCHIE. Well, not in this country they don't.

WANDA. Oh right, like nobody lies in England . . . like Margaret Thatcher never lies.

ARCHIE. Look, you lied to me right from the moment we met, right from . . .

WANDA (*interrupting him*). Oh come on, Archie, you just wanted to get me into bed.

ARCHIE. I fell in love with you.

Wanda turns and looks at him. A pause.

WANDA. How come you dumped me, then?

ARCHIE. I wasn't rich enough, remember?

A flicker of a smile crosses his face. Wanda looks at him quizzically. She leans across to him.

WANDA. Say something in Russian.

ARCHIE (*pretending to be cross*). No!

  Cut to:

120. Exterior. London street. Day.

Archie's Jaguar is moving faster.

  Cut to:

121. Interior. Archie's car. Day.

The mood has changed. Archie has his arm round Wanda, who is cuddling up to him.

WANDA. What are you thinking, Archie?

ARCHIE. I'm just trying to think of one good reason why I should take you to South America with me.

WANDA. How about . . . because I have the key to the safety-deposit box.

ARCHIE AND WANDA (*in unison*). That's a good reason.

They both laugh.

Cut to:

122. Exterior. George's block. Day.

Archie's car screams up to the curb.

WANDA. What do we do about Otto?

ARCHIE. I'll handle Otto.

WANDA. Be careful, he's dangerous.

Archie kisses her.

ARCHIE. So am I.

He leaps out of the car.

Keep it running.

He sprints into Kipling Mansions. Suddenly Otto appears from nowhere and jumps into the car.

OTTO. Why did you bring him?

WANDA. Otto! Otto, just wait!

OTTO. I'm beginning to think you like that creature.

WANDA. Otto, just wait a minute, OK?

OTTO. No! Let's get the diamonds.

Cut to:

123. Interior. George's flat. Day.

Archie flies in and is astonished by the sight of Ken, who is lying on the floor, tied to the stool. The chips have been removed but the pear is in his mouth and he cannot speak.

ARCHIE. Ken? Are you Ken?

Archie sees the pear and removes it. Ken gasps. Archie starts untying him.

How d'you do. I'm George's barrister. What's happened?

Suddenly there is a crash from outside. Archie runs to the window.

Oh my God.

Cut to:

124. Exterior. George's block. Day.

Otto, in pulling out, has caused an accident. The other driver has got out of his car and is advancing on Otto, remonstrating. Otto rolls the window down, and fires a shot, knocking the driver's hat off. The driver runs for his life. Otto waves up at Archie and drives off. Wanda shouts out of the window.

WANDA. Archie!

Cut to:

125. Interior. George's flat. Day.

Archie struggles with his amazement and turns to Ken.

ARCHIE. Where have they gone!? Quick! Where have they gone?

KEN (*recovering*). They've g . . . they've ggg . . .

ARCHIE. What?

KEN. The . . . ggg ...

ARCHIE. Are you all right? Where have they gone?

KEN. They've gone to the Cath . . . c . . .

ARCHIE. Are you ill?

KEN. Nn . . . they gg . . . t . . .

ARCHIE. Have you got a stutter?

KEN (*nodding*). Y . . . a bbbbbbbbi . . . bi . . .

ARCHIE. (*calmly*). OK, fine. Don't worry. Do you know where they've gone?

KEN. Y . . . Y . . .

ARCHIE. Fine, fine. Where?

KEN. The Ccaa . . . Hotel.

ARCHIE. Hotel? Which hotel?

The Ccc . . . the Ccc . . . the Cc . . . c . . .

Ken's attempt to say 'Cathcart Towers' is a record-breaking stutter.

ARCHIE. All right, wait, wait, wait . . . Slowly, very slowly.

Archie waits, agonized, while Ken tries to get the words out.

No hurry. It's OK.

Still no success.

Sing it.

(*in a high-pitched voice*). The Caa . . . the Ca . . .

ARCHIE. Plenty of time.

KEN (*higher*). The Cc . . . the Caa . . .

ARCHIE. (*suddenly desperate*) Oh, *come on!* (*immediately repents*) I'm sorry . . . sorry . . . wait . . .

Ken keeps trying as Archie runs over to the table, picks up a pen and gives it to Ken.

Here, write it.

Ken grabs a newspaper from the floor and writes 'CATHCART TOWERS HOTEL'.

Cathcart Towers Hotel?

Ken nods.

KEN. Cathcart Towers Hotel.

Ken is amazed at himself.

ARCHIE. Well, where is it? Ken, where is it? Where?

KEN. Hea . . . Hea . . .

Archie offers him the pen but Ken insists on miming a plane taking off.

ARCHIE (*inspiration*). Heathrow Airport.

   Cut to:

126. Exterior. London streets. Day.

Ken hurtles along on his motorcycle with Archie clinging on behind.

   Cut to:

127. Exterior. Cathcart Towers Hotel. Day.

Archie's car screeches to a halt right outside the doors to the hotel. Otto and Wanda leap out. An astonished hotel porter tries to stop them.

HOTEL PORTER. Hey! What's the idea? You can't . . .

OTTO (*English accent*). Excuse me, terribly sorry. Take it, it's yours.

   They run inside.

   Cut to:

128. Exterior. Street by Heathrow Airport. Day.

Ken and Archie whizz along on the motorcycle. In the distance, a plane takes off.

   Cut to:

129. Interior. Security box area. Cathcart Towers Hotel. Day.

Otto and Wanda conclude their business with the reception clerk. Wanda takes a black bag from the safety deposit box and puts it into her hand luggage.

   OTTO. Thank you so much. British Airways to Rio?

   RECEPTION CLERK. Rio? Terminal 4, sir.

WANDA. Thank you.

They rush off.

Cut to:

130. Exterior. Cathcart Towers Hotel. Day.

Ken's motorcycle skids to a halt, and Archie sees his car illegally parked, surrounded by a traffic warden and a policeman. He runs to it, leans in and takes the passport out of the briefcase.

POLICEMAN. Excuse me sir, is this your vehicle?

ARCHIE. I'll be with you in a moment. I'll be right back.

He runs into the hotel after Ken.

Cut to:

131. Interior. Airport check-in area. Day.

Wanda looks up at the Rio flight details on the information board, as Otto checks in.

AIRLINE EMPLOYEE. Aisle or window, smoking or non-smoking?

OTTO. What was the middle one . . .?

WANDA. Anything in non-smoking is fine, thank you.

AIRLINE EMPLOYEE. Gate 14 is boarding now.

They hurry off.

Cut to:

132. Interior. Cathcart Towers lobby. Day.

Ken and Archie look around frantically. Then run off towards the check-in area.

Cut to:

133. Interior. Airport Security. Day.

Otto manages to smuggle his gun through the security scanning-gate by throwing it round and catching it the other side. He picks up Wanda's hand luggage as it emerges from the luggage rack, to her annoyance.

Cut to:

134. Interior. Airport check-in area. Day.

Archie and Ken look around hopelessly. No sign of their quarry. Ken suddenly tugs at Archie's arm and points above a distant check-in desk.

Their POV: A sign reading: 'BA313 – RIO DE JANEIRO'.

We hear the final call for the British Airways flight to Rio de Janeiro.

ARCHIE. Rio!

He hurries to the British Airways desk.

Cut to:

135. Interior. Long corridors leading to departure lounges. Day.

Wanda and Otto hurry along. Suddenly Wanda looks alarmed.

WANDA. Don't look round but there's a cop right behind us.

They turn a corner and as Otto peers round to look for the cops, Wanda coshes him.

Cut to:

136. Interior. Airport check-in area. Day.

Archie waits to see whether there are any seats available on the Rio flight.

AIRLINE EMPLOYEE. Yes, we can just do it, Mr Leach.

ARCHIE. Great.

AIRLINE EMPLOYEE. Luggage?

Archie suddenly sees Ken on a luggage belt, disappearing down a chute. Archie is startled. The employee looks at him, enquiringly.

ARCHIE. Don't . . . really need any.

AIRLINE EMPLOYEE. Gate 14.

She hands him his ticket. Archie rushes off.

Cut to:

137. Interior. Corridor leading to departure lounge. Day.

Wanda crams the rest of Otto into a broom cupboard, and locks it. She stuffs the cupboard key and Otto's boarding pass into a nearby trash can.

WANDA. *Ciao, stupidissimo.*

Cut to:

138. Exterior. Baggage-handling chute. Day.

Ken is having a rough journey, spiralling down the baggage chute. Suitcases overtake him.

Cut to:

139. Interior. Airport Security. Day.

Archie runs through the security scanners at full speed.

Cut to:

140. Exterior. Baggage-handling area. Day.

Ken lands in a crumpled heap at the bottom of the chute and manages to disentangle himself. He gets up, looks around, and runs off.

Cut to:

141. Interior. Corridor leading to departure lounge. Day.

An Indian cleaner is sweeping near Otto's cupboard, talking to herself. A silenced revolver starts shooting away the lock. The cleaner takes no notice. Otto bursts out of the cupboard and runs off, knocking over some of the cleaner's brooms.

Cut to:

142. Interior. Departure lounge. Day.

Wanda is on the telephone in a payphone booth. She looks very fraught.

WANDA. Come on, Archie, pick up the phone.

Cut to:

143. Interior. Corridor leading to departure lounge. Day.

Archie rounds a corner, almost knocking over the Indian cleaner, and sees Otto running off in the distance.

Cut to:

144. Interior. Departure lounge. Day.

Getting no reply from Archie's number, Wanda slams down the phone in frustration. She hurries off.

Cut to:

145. Interior. Another airport corridor. Day.

Otto approaches a late arrival, Hutchison.

OTTO. Excuse me, sir. Airport Security. May I see your boarding pass please?

HUTCHISON. Oh, certainly.

OTTO. Very good. Now would you mind stepping over here please. Oh look, the Queen. (*he points down the corridor*)

HUTCHISON. Where?

Otto bonks Hutchison on the head with his gun, puts it on the floor and starts hauling Hutchison out of sight. Archie comes round the corner and can hardly believe his luck. He picks up the gun, and sticks it in Otto's ribs as he straightens up. Otto stiffens.

OTTO. OK, OK, don't get excited.

Archie pushes him down the corridor and round a corner. He shoves him up against some doors.
Otto turns round nervously and sees Archie.

Oh! It's you. I was actually worried there for a moment.

He takes his hands down.

ARCHIE. Keep your hands up.

OTTO. No.

ARCHIE. Put them up.

OTTO. I'll make a deal with you, I'll put one up.

Otto puts one arm up.

ARCHIE Put the other one up.

Otto puts the other one up but takes the first one down.

OTTO. Which looks better?

He alternates raised arms experimentally.

ARCHIE. I'm warning you, Otto . . .

OTTO. What are you going to do, Archie? Shoot me? Gun me down in cold blood like a dog? Hey! If you want to settle something with me, then why don't you fight me? You're a man, aren't you, Archie? Then let's fight like men. Come on!

Otto adopts the Queensberry pose. Archie stares.

ARCHIE. . . . All right.

OTTO. All right then.

ARCHIE. OK.

Archie puts the gun down and they circle.

OTTO. You look good, Arch.

ARCHIE. That's right, Otto. I used to box for Oxford.

OTTO. Oh yeah? Well, I used to kill for the CIA.

He picks the gun off the floor and points it at Archie.

Now . . . get your hands up.

ARCHIE. No.

Otto fires two shots, which rip the shoulder pads off Archie's jacket. Archie looks alarmed and puts his hands up.

OTTO. You spineless bimbo. Now, out.

He indicates. Archie goes through the door.

Cut to:

146. Exterior. Taxiing area. Day.

They come out on to the taxiing area. It's fairly deserted, bar a British Airways jumbo. The cement is being resurfaced and wooden planks have been laid down to walk on. Among all this is a large barrel of black goo. Archie and Otto are teetering along the planks towards it.

OTTO. OK, I'm going to have to shoot you now, Archie. But er, I've got a little time before my plane leaves and I'm longing to humiliate you. So get in that barrel.

Archie looks at it.

ARCHIE. What?

OTTO. In the barrel.

Archie continues to look disbelievingly at the barrel. Otto fires a shot at his crotch. Archie gets in with haste.

You English! You think you're so superior, don't you. Well, you're the filth of the planet. A bunch of pompous, badly-dressed, poverty-stricken, sexually repressed football hooligans . . .

While Otto is insulting him, Archie looks up and sees, to his amazement, a steamroller coming towards them. Ken is driving it. Otto takes aim with his gun.

Goodbye, Archie.

Archie thinks fast.

ARCHIE. Well, at least we're not irretrievably vulgar.

OTTO. You know your problem? You don't like winners.

ARCHIE. Winners?

OTTO. Yeah, *winners*.

ARCHIE. Winners like . . . North Vietnam?

OTTO. Shut up! We did not lose Vietnam. It was a tie.

In the background, Ken is slowly bearing down on Otto.

ARCHIE (*in bad American accent*). I'm tellin' ya, baby, they kicked your little ass there. Boy, they whopped your hide real good.

OTTO. No they didn't.

ARCHIE. Oh yes they did.

OTTO. Oh no they didn't.

ARCHIE. Oh yes they did.

OTTO. Oh no they d . . . shut up. Goodbye, Archie.

He aims his gun at Archie.

ARCHIE. Going to shoot me?

OTTO (*English accent*). Yes, 'fraid so, old chap. Sorry!

The steamroller is very near. Archie suddenly points at it.

ARCHIE. Look, Otto. Look!

Otto turns round and does a double-take on Ken.

KEN. Rev . . . enge!

Otto is very amused indeed. He laughs and laughs and as he does so he takes several steps back off the wooden planks onto the wet cement.

OTTO. Ah ha ha ha. It's Kkkken cccoming to kkkkill me. How you going to ccccatch me, Kkkken?

He laughs, then remembers Archie.

Now, where was I?

He turns back to Archie, but something is wrong. He cannot turn round properly. He looks down and sees that his feet are stuck in the wet cement. He tries to move them. He can't. Archie registers what is happening in disbelief.

Shit! Fucking limey cement.

Otto starts to panic. He fires at Ken but it bounces off the steamroller. He fires again but there are no more bullets left. He throws the gun away. Archie is getting out of the barrel.

Ken! Ken! Wait! Kenny . . . may I call you Kenny?

KEN. Remember Wanda!

OTTO. I've got the deal of a lifetime. 50-50 you and me, what do you say? OK, OK, 60–40, it's my final offer.

KEN. Revenge!

OTTO. Wait, I've got an idea, you take it all. Here's my boarding pass.

Ken is now very close.

KEN. I'm going to kkk . . . I'm going to kkkill you.

OTTO (*trying a different tack*). OK, fine, Ken. Come at me. Give me your best shot. Go on, Ken, you don't have the guts, admit it.

The steamroller is only yards away.

OK, you have the guts. Good. Wait.

KEN. Death!

OTTO. All right, I'm sorry I ate your fish. OK? I'm sorry.

KEN (*almost upon him*). Revenge!

OTTO. Jesus, I said I'm sorry, what the fu . . .

He screams horribly as the steamroller sucks him under.

KEN. Got him!

Archie, who is now out of the barrel, watches in amazement, as Ken turns the steamroller round to go over Otto again. He makes a dash for the British Airways plane.

Ken stands triumphantly at the wheel of the steamroller, shouting gleefully.

Got you again. You bastard! Hey, I've lost my stutter, it's gone.

I can speak! How much wood would a woodchuck chuck if a woodchuck could chuck wood. Ha ha ha ha!

Ken runs over what looks like a patch of strawberry yoghurt again. Various folk and vehicles run towards Ken and his roller.

Cut to:

147. Interior. Entrance of plane BA 313. Day.

Archie boards the plane, looking very dishevelled.

BRITISH AIRWAYS STEWARD. Good afternoon, sir. Boarding pass?

Archie hands it to him and looks down the aisles.

Wanda is in a window seat, staring reflectively into the distance. Archie appears and sits beside her.

ARCHIE. *Buongiorno, signorina.*

Wanda looks round, sees him and throws her arms round him, hugging him. They kiss.

Now listen, two things. One, behave yourself from now on or I'll break your neck, OK. Two, Gorbachev, Glasnost . . .

WANDA. Molotov . . .

They laugh.

ARCHIE. Blinis . . .

WANDA. Ah, Lenin . . .

As they speak, a figure appears at the window, peering inside at the two of them. The figure is covered in cement.

ARCHIE. Pushkin . . .

WANDA. Chicken kiev . . .

ARCHIE. Good . . . Dostoevsky . . .

The cement-man, looking remarkably like Otto, mouthes 'Asshole' at the window.

WANDA. Roubles . . .

She takes Archie's hand in hers. The cement-man is looking horrified.

ARCHIE. Vladivostok . . .

The plane's engines start up and the figure at the window is flung backwards out of sight.

OTTO. Asshole!

Cut to:

148. Exterior. Heathrow Airport. Day.

A British Airways jumbo takes off. The plane flies off into the distance.

FIN

Subsequently:

Archie and Wanda were married in Rio, had seventeen children, and founded a leper colony.

Ken became Master of Ceremonies at the London Sea World.

Otto emigrated to South Africa and became Minister for Justice.